FOREST GREEN

ALSO BY KATE PULLINGER

KATE PULLINGER

FOREST GREEN

DOUBLEDAY CANADA

Doubleday Canada and colophon are registered trademarks of Penguin Random House Canada Limited

Library and Archives Canada Cataloguing in Publication

Title: Forest green / Kate Pullinger.
Names: Pullinger, Kate, author.
Identifiers: Canadiana (print) 20190158786 | Canadiana (ebook) 20190158875 | ISBN 9780385683043 (hardcover) | ISBN 9780385683050 (EPUB)
Classification: LCC PS8581.U46 F67 2020 | DDC C813/.54—dc23

This book is a work of fiction. Names, characters, places and incidents are products of the author's imagination or are used fictitiously. Any resemblance to actual events or locales or persons, living or dead, is entirely coincidental.

Jacket and book design: Leah Springate
Jacket images: (boy) SimonSkafar, (texture) Katsumi Murouchi, both Getty Images; (clouds) John Hult, (sky) Fahrul Azmi, both Unsplash

Printed and bound in Canada

Published in Canada by Doubleday Canada, a division of Penguin Random House Canada Limited

www.penguinrandomhouse.ca

10 9 8 7 6 5 4 3 2 1

Penguin
Random House
DOUBLEDAY CANADA

For Marilee Sigal, traveller extraordinaire

"It is hard, even now, to imagine the magnitude of the timber coming out of these woods throughout the nineteenth and twentieth centuries."

—FROM *The Golden Spruce* BY JOHN VAILLANT

1995: Sawdust

A KICK TO THE RIBS. Brutal. Violent. No—just the shock of waking once again. The pain low in his back, sharp then dull then sharp again.

It stung to breathe. His lungs soaked in it—the heavy wet air sitting like a monkey on his chest. A monkey?

Tied up—was he tied up? Was he tied to a tree? A skinny old pine tree? Was he in the jungle? Was Peg nearby? No. Art battled to the surface through layers of memory. A blanket was twisted around his legs, restricting his movement, and beneath that he could feel the metal grid of the doorstep through the soggy cardboard. Everything was wet except his mouth, which was dry—parched. Lips crusted and cracked. Sore. Everything. Sore. He patted his pocket—no glasses. And he had a black eye—was it a black eye? Swollen shut. He'd hit his head, he'd fallen over and hit his head and now that side of his face felt pulpy. His fingers came away tacky with blood.

No idea of the time. It sounded like morning, seagulls and traffic. Beyond that, Art could hear the harbour, he could smell sea salt in the air. Even now, he knew he could head down to the water, walk out on a log boom, knock on the door of the harbour office, and land a job. Get out of the damned city and back to the forest. Back to the towering trees. Back to the salal with its black berries, the pillowy moss, and the deep dark quiet of the woods at night.

But not just now. Not today.

Somebody had left a burger for him in a paper bag. With fries. The smell was greasy, sickening, but it brought him round, back to his senses. If he sat up, he knew he'd start retching. Retching and shaking; sometimes he shook so bad he was his own personal earthquake. But he should eat. He knew he should eat. He couldn't remember the last time he'd eaten. He knew he shouldn't be lying there, tangled up in a blanket in a doorway in a puddle of—what? He should be dry, sheltered— A puddle of piss. Whose piss?

And if he sat up, he didn't know how much control over his arms and legs he'd have. It was more than the shakes—it was as though his body had a will of its own these days. Prone to flailing, legs giving way, his insides rattling like a tin with a few coins in it. He had no cash, he didn't hold on to cash, the junkies were ruthless and he'd been rolled a few times before he got wise. His pension—what day was it? If he could get up he could go over to that place on Hastings, they knew him down there, they'd let him wash up, help him find a bed, he'd . . .

Art rolled over onto his back. The clouds were low and the

air was frigid and . . . what was that, falling from the sky? Snow? He stuck out his tongue and took a flake into his mouth. But it wasn't snow. It was sawdust. He'd heard the volunteer workers used sawdust to keep people from freezing. When the shelters were full and they ran out of those silver heat blankets, they went around in an old logging truck and shovelled heaps of sawdust onto people while they slept, to keep them warm, to stop them dying.

The sawdust stung his battered eye. He raised his hand to brush it away.

Peg. It comforted him to think of his sister. He hadn't seen her for a long time, not since he borrowed that money. After that, he hadn't been able to face her, and not just because he owed her. He was waiting 'til he got his act together. 'Til he had a place, was on an even keel. He wanted to return home the big guy, full of stories, flush with money, a great wad of cash to pay back Peg and Frank, a room full of people all happy to see him, flowers for the women, whiskey for the men. But he'd been this way for a while now. How long? Down on his luck. He'd been this way.

Things would get better. They always had. He'd run into someone he knew, he'd convince someone, somewhere, to give him a job. Bussing tables, bagging groceries, sweeping the sidewalk. He'd find a camp he could call home. He'd find a jungle.

Was it sawdust? No—snow. Vancouver snow, claggy and wet, like a sugar-free slushie from the corner store, spilling from the sky.

His chest ached. The pain in his lower back pulsed as though there was something in there waking up, wanting to get out. He needed to piss. But the thought of having to get up defeated him.

Art closed his eyes.

Flashing blue and red lights. Voices.

Best to pretend to be asleep. Best to hope whoever it was would pass on by. Though a night in the clink wasn't such a bad idea. A night in the clink might be just the thing.

"What's up, old buddy?"

Art didn't reply.

"Come on, buddy. There's an ambulance here for you."

Art opened his eyes. There was a small crowd of people standing in the street, paramedics with a stretcher, and a young bearded guy wearing a dirty old Cowichan sweater and a John Deere cap standing right over him, one of those do-gooder types.

"Come on, old man. What's your name?" he said.

My name, thought Art. My name? It's all that's left of me. Arthur Lunn, he thought, Art Lunn, that's me. But his mouth wouldn't open. He was too weighed down by the cold wet air. He couldn't speak.

1934: The Jungle

THE FLOW OF MEN COMING THROUGH town looking for work had grown and grown until it was like a river, laden with debris, bumping and tumbling, carving new channels. Hobos. Art rolled the word round his mouth. They used to knock on the door asking for work—odd jobs around the house and yard—but Art's mother never had any jobs to hand out, what with four kids to do chores. And then, as though word had spread, the men stopped asking for work and moved on to asking for handouts. They stood at the back door of the house, clutching their hats, and some of them looked so ashamed it was painful to see. Art's mother did what she could, parcelling out leftovers, taking Art's big sister Tilly with her to help out down at the soup kitchen when she could spare the time.

And now, according to the grown-ups, there was a jungle on the edge of town. A jungle where the hobos were living.

Art had heard his father talking about it with Archie Portman's father in church. Art had been sitting between his father and his sister Peg, who'd told him off for fidgeting, but it was hot and his shirt was stuck to his back and he was bored though the service hadn't even started yet. Art contemplated the back of his friend Archie's head in the next pew: red curly hair that was ripe for tugging. And then his father leaned forward to talk to Mr. Portman.

"A jungle," his father said.

The word caught Art's attention.

"Yep," said Mr. Portman. "Our very own."

"Whose land is it?" his father asked.

"Templeton's," replied Mr. Portman. "Says he can't do anything about it. Says the ravine is useless anyway."

Peg elbowed Art in the side.

"Move over," she whispered.

"Shh. They're talking about a jungle."

Peg's eyes widened.

"He feels he should turn a blind eye," Mr. Portman added.

"Why on earth would he think that?" their father asked.

"A bit of Christian charity? Earning his place in the hereafter?" Mr. Portman gave a shrug. "Your guess is as good as mine."

"There really is a jungle?" Art whispered to Peg.

"There really is," Peg replied, her eyes wide.

And Art knew without either of them saying another word that he and Peg were going to find it.

—

School had finished last week, finally—it had gone on forever and ever this year. Their mother had kept the four of them occupied since then with all manner of tasks, even Eddie the baby had a job sorting lids and bands for the jam jars. She'd had Art beating carpets yesterday; she'd strung them up on the clothesline and they'd bowed the line down, almost touching the ground. It was odd to see the familiar textures and patterns hanging outside in the sun. Art enjoyed it—not that he would admit it—whacking the rugs with the big broom, raising up a huge cloud of dust. He could still taste the dirt at the back of his mouth, scratchy in his throat when he swallowed. Better than being stuck inside, like Peg, at the sewing machine.

Today was their first day of true freedom. They'd finished their chores early and quickly and made their escape before their mother had a chance to inspect their work, before the day grew too hot to move. They were going to find the jungle. Art knew where it was, or, he thought he knew where it might be; he knew where the Templeton orchards were, at least.

The lake was as still as a bucket of water, heat shimmying off the dusty road that ran along the beach. Art trotted behind Peg; why was she always so much faster than him? He'd catch up one day. They walked past the railway roundhouse, skirting wide—there were more than a hundred men living there, according to Art's father; their number had grown steadily over the winter and now the place was bursting. The railway company let the men use the roundhouse as a shelter, provided they didn't interfere with the running of the turntable. Art's dad didn't like it, he'd told Mr. Portman he thought they were a hazard, and he couldn't understand why the company would tolerate all those men occupying their property.

"There's too many of them now—the railway couldn't move them on if they wanted to," Mr. Portman had said.

Why the men would live there when they could live in a jungle was beyond Art, but he found grown-ups mostly baffling. He'd been down to the roundhouse once with Archie to see what there was to see, even though his mother had told him to stay away. Turned out there wasn't much to watch, just a lot of raggedy-looking men coming and going. Archie claimed that inside it was like a Chinese laundry, they used the roundhouse stove to boil their underwear, and they cooked soup on it as well, and at night the hobos lay on the floor to sleep in orderly rows, everyone turning over at the same time.

Art followed Peg along the railway line, jumping over the rails, avoiding the ties freshly soaked in creosote. The town ended quickly. Art wanted to remain on the tracks as they cut up through the hillside—he liked walking along the tracks, knowing they led to his father.

"But that's the wrong direction," Peg said, and Art knew she was right.

Peg was usually right. She was one whole year older than him, eight to his seven, and one whole year smarter as well. Art knew he should be doing this with Archie, who was his best pal. Archie, with his wild hair that he claimed had never been touched by brush or comb, and his layers and layers upon layers of freckles. Archie would be hopping mad when he heard Art had found the jungle without him. But the truth was if you wanted to get something done you were better off asking Peg. It was annoying, but she was unaccountably brave. Just yesterday their mother had sent her out to kill one of the chickens and Peg had snapped its neck like she was snapping a twig. When he was with her, Art was brave too.

They walked through what remained of the old railway workers' cottages, which were really no more than glorified lean-tos as far as Art could see; he found it difficult to believe his parents had ever lived in one. The house they lived in now—the house his father had built—was a palace in comparison.

Art was looking forward to the day he'd be old enough to go to work with his father. Dad left home on Monday morning and returned on Friday afternoon most weeks, layered with coal dust and creosote and sweat. He worked up and down the Kettle Valley Railway line, wherever the bridge-and-tunnel crew was needed. He'd promised Art that when he was ten—his mum said twelve, but his dad had said ten, and that's what Art was sticking with—he could start spending his summers working with the railway crew. He'd learn to drive the handcar, and he'd be able to pump it up the line faster than anybody, he was sure. But he wouldn't be ten for ages.

The spring had been hotter and drier than normal and the cherry harvest was underway already. This year the farm workers were camping out among the trees, due to the scale of pilfering.

"They've got guns," Peg had warned him as they'd set out that morning.

"Guns?" Art had replied.

"Rifles. Shotguns." She gave her head a little shake, which Art knew meant she wasn't entirely confident in her story. "We need to be careful not to startle them. They might mistake us for hobos. We might get shot."

But there was little chance of that happening; Art had his father's canteen slung around his neck and two tin mugs dangling off that, and they made a racket with every step he took.

"That'll scare away the snakes," Peg had said by way of convincing him that he was the one who ought to carry them.

She was full of information about the rattlesnakes in the hills above the lake, about the farmhand who had stepped backwards unaware, flushing the snake out of its lair.

"He got bit," Peg said. "He died."

Sometimes at night when Art was lying in bed he'd hear the wind hissing through the trees at the end of their street, rattling the branches, as though an enormous serpent was making its way through town. He'd never believed the stories about the monster that lived in the dark depths of the lake, but the stories of the rattlers, well, he knew for sure they were true. He'd seen enough snakeskins; in fact, most of his friends had snakeskins they displayed like trophies, keeping them folded up in their fathers' old hankies in their back pockets until the skins crumpled and fell apart. Last summer, Archie found a snakeskin that was more than five feet long.

He spent several days showing it off as though it was evidence of his own shape-shifting. It turned out to belong to a rattlesnake that was living in the crawl space under the Portmans' house; their dog Jolly discovered it one day and got bit in the process. Archie's dad, Mr. Portman, killed the rattler and then the poor poisoned dog with a shovel while Archie screamed so loudly the whole street came out to see what was happening. Art took one look at the dead dog with its crushed skull and retreated to his own front steps, while his friends paraded past to inspect the carnage. The grown-ups insisted later that it was a freak occurrence, that rattlers were shy and normally stayed well away from town, only striking out when cornered—and even then, if you stood still, the snake would usually calm down and slither away. The little dog hadn't had this information.

Art was afraid of rattlesnakes, but as the possibility that they might actually find the jungle increased, Art realized with a shudder that it was even more frightening to him. Just the word on its own. Jungle.

It was a hobo camp. That was all Art knew. There was a big one down in Vancouver, Art's mother read about it in the newspaper. And now their town had one of its own. The grown-ups didn't like it; they'd held a meeting in town to discuss what to do about it. According to Art's mother, there had been a good deal of disagreement. When she got home she said to Art's father, "These men have to rest somewhere, and why not here, where it's warm and the trees are dense with fruit instead of pine cones?"

Only last week Mr. Portman had come across the street to discuss it with Art's father.

"There's too many of them now," Mr. Portman had said. "We should run them out."

The two men sat on the top step of the front porch. Art took his place beside his father.

"Templeton's gone soft in the head. They belong in the relief camps." Mr. Portman owned the grocery store on Main Street and was keen on what he referred to as "our civic duty."

"Well, they're not doing anyone any harm, are they? They're only trying to get by—there but for the grace of God," Art's dad replied.

Art knew that his family was lucky—his dad had a good job, they had food on their table, shoes on their feet. Of course he knew, how could he not—it was something his parents had hammered into him like it was gospel. And in a way, it was. Four children, and all of them healthy. Count your blessings before they get taken away.

"Those men," Art's dad said, "they're no different from you or me."

They were in one of Templeton's orchards now. Peg was up ahead, jumping over the irrigation flumes and furrows, moving through the stony orchard like a goat, compact and sure-footed. Finding the jungle had been Art's idea, but she'd latched onto it as though he was some kind of genius, and they'd made it their joint project. Art had no idea what they'd do if they actually found it; he hoped at the very least it would make a good story to tell his friends, one to rival Archie's rattlesnake.

The trees around Art were heavy with fruit, the ground so parched it was as though the peaches had sucked up all the available water and were storing it inside their flesh. Another month or so and the whole town would be drenched in sweetness as the smell of fruit ripening drifted down from the orchards and out from the countless kitchens where an annual canning spree took place. Canning was one of the only times his father helped out in the kitchen; all that boiling water and steam was familiar territory for him, he said. This year it had been so warm for so long already that the early peaches were nearly ready, and now that Art was in the orchard, the smell of the fruit was slowing him down, making him feel like he was moving through syrup.

Art loved peaches. Fresh, canned, in pies, in cakes, in jam. Of all the fruit in the Okanagan—cherries, apricots, apples, plums—he loved peaches best. Yellow peaches, with a red blush, eaten on the grass near the water so you could run into the lake afterwards when you were covered in juice, escape from the ants and the wasps and wash yourself down. There was even a town called Peachland along the lake; Art thought he might like to live there one day. Peg always insisted on peeling the skin off hers. She had this idea that if you ate the skin you might choke to death on it; she claimed she'd heard about a girl in Vernon who had died that way. Art was too impatient to peel a peach. The workers usually picked the fruit before it was ripe so it was easier to pack and ship, but the fruit in this orchard hadn't been harvested yet, and these peaches looked perfect. Right now he longed to put aside his worries about snakes, to forget about this quest to find the jungle, to pick a peach and sit down right here on the hillside and eat it. He stopped to take a drink of water from his dad's flask, not bothering to use the tin mug, Peg too far ahead to tell him off. He felt a bit swoony.

He took another swig. Someone was watching him, he felt it. He turned quickly, the tin mugs clattering. At the end of the long row of trees was a man, holding something—a gun, Art thought, or maybe it was a stick. Art couldn't tell if the man was a farm worker or a hobo—they dressed the same, more or less, sweaty and dirty. In fact, they often were the same, at least according to Art's dad—the hope of seasonal work in the orchards was why so many men had come to the Okanagan. The man was watching Art. Art stared back. He wasn't sure what to do. The man probably knew he had been about to steal a peach.

He heard Peg calling in the distance. "Hurry up, Art! Come on!"

He took off running.

When he caught up with her, she had a peach in one hand. She held it up and he could see she'd peeled away a patch of skin and taken a bite.

"Not ripe," she said, and she put on an extravagant pout. "Very sad."

She handed the peach to Art and he hauled back and chucked it as hard as he could in the direction of the lake.

Peg whispered, "Splash."

They were out of the orchards now, on a broad bench of land that rose above the orderly rows of fruit trees with their cargo of sweetness. Here the trees were sparse and skinny, and Art felt a little safer, less likely to run into anybody. They'd passed the graveyard a while back, lower down the slope. Art was relieved that Peg hadn't pointed it out; she claimed to love the graveyard and was forever trying to convince him it was a place they should sneak out at night to visit.

"It's hot," Art complained when they paused, looking at the lake below.

"It's hot because it's semi-arid," Peg announced.

"Do you remember everything those teachers tell you?"

"Yes."

"'Semi-arid.'"

"It's like a desert, but not quite."

Art scoffed. "Semi-my-derrière," he replied.

Peg laughed, like he knew she would.

The going was tough. They were on a footpath that cut along the side of the hill, and the ground was uneven and crumbly, prone to shifting beneath their feet. They were surrounded by blackberry brambles and prickly bushes— everything sharp and spiky, liable to lash out when they weren't expecting it. Art was wearing short trousers and his bare skin was scratched and bleeding a little, but he didn't care. There was a road up above but Peg said she figured they wouldn't be able to see the jungle from there, and, besides, someone from town might stop them and ask where they were heading.

"Is this really the right way?" Art asked, though he knew Peg didn't know the answer.

"Who do you think made this footpath? It's not as though anyone else would come up here," Peg said over her shoulder.

"Who d'you think made this footpath?" Art whispered to himself in a snidey voice. He wished he could turn around and go back home but he knew Peg would tell everyone he'd been too afraid to continue. There was no escape.

Peg had stopped at the crest of the hill, and Art scrambled to catch up with her. They were on the rim of a steep ravine— a dark green slash in the brown hillside. Art looked toward the lake and saw that the ravine broadened out there into a tidy lush field, luminous against the dry brown earth that surrounded it.

"Look." Peg was pointing down into the ravine.

And there it was. The jungle.

Art couldn't believe he hadn't seen it straightaway. It was a decrepit-looking collection of lean-tos and bivouacs, constructed from tin sheeting, canvas tarps, broken-down apple crates and brushweed. It teemed with men. Even from here Art could see how busy it was. There were several small fires burning, thin smoke trails moving skyward. Some men were sitting around the fires, cooking, some moving around the camp, while others were lying flat out on the ground with their hats pulled down over their faces, sleeping in the middle of the day. Sleeping in the middle of the day!

It didn't look anything like how Art had imagined. Of course he knew it was a hobo camp, and that it wouldn't necessarily be a jungle just because people called it that. He knew Tarzan wouldn't be living there. But he realized now as he looked down at it that a part of him had been hoping there'd be ropes to swing from, and green pools of water to jump into, and maybe, just maybe, a monkey to play with. He didn't think it was unreasonable to suppose a hobo might be accompanied by a monkey. He kicked the dirt, embarrassed. At least he hadn't told Peg about the monkey.

"There's a lot of them," she said, and her voice sounded small.

"Yes," said Art.

Peg took Art's hand. He didn't mind.

They heard a sound behind them on the footpath, and they both whirled round. The man Art had seen in the orchard was standing right there, close enough to reach out and grab them. He was tall and thin with hollow cheeks and a scraggly beard; his brow jutted out, casting his eyes into shade. His extra-long fingers made Art think of the white spiders he'd seen coming out of a drain behind the school one day. The man smelled bad, and he looked hungry.

"What are you kids up to?" he asked.

Art waited for Peg to reply. She didn't.

"We're playing," Art said.

"You're not playing. You're spying."

"No, we—"

"Someone from town sent you."

"Nobody sent us," Art said. "Nobody knows we're here." As soon as he said it, he knew he shouldn't have.

"You shouldn't be out here. It's dangerous. You should go on home."

That woke Peg up; she didn't like to be told what to do.

"We can go wherever we like," she said. "You can't tell us what to do."

It didn't take much to make Peg indignant, but Art had never heard her speak to a grown-up that way.

The man laughed, but not in a nice way. "Have you got anything to eat?" he asked.

Peg put her hand on her satchel. "No," she lied.

Art looked from Peg to the man. Then, in a series of swift, sure moves, the man reached down, picked Art up, slung him over his shoulder like a butcher with a side of beef, and took off, running down the hill toward the jungle. Art—bouncing hard, the pressure on his stomach from the man's shoulder something awful—lifted his head and saw that Peg was chasing them down the hill, shouting a blue streak.

"You stop right there, you stop that, you put him down!"

He wanted to tell Peg to run back to town to get help, but he had no voice, as though it had been jolted out of him when he was thrown over the man's shoulder.

He knew, he knew with terrible certainty, that when they

reached the jungle, he and Peg would both be captured and killed. And, maybe, eaten.

Moments later, the man slowed to a stop and swung Art down to the ground. Art slowly patted himself down, checking that all his parts were still attached. They were at the edge of the encampment. If there had been an entrance, a door or gate, this is where it would have stood, but of course there was nothing like that. As Art gulped air, trying to catch his breath, his nostrils filled with an awful stench, like nothing he had ever smelled before. It smelled of burning—campfires, cooking—and dirt and sweat and . . . and what? The smell of men. The overpowering smell of a great gang of unwashed men, all crowded together in this ravine. It was the jungle smell, Art realized.

Art looked up at the man, but the sun was directly overhead and so his face was blacked out. Where was Peg? He turned to look for her but as he did the man clamped a hand on his arm. Art opened his mouth to shout, but before he could, he was back over the man's shoulder.

He would be cooked. He would be eaten.

When the man put him down again they were next to a firepit. The fire was producing acrid fumes—creosote. Art looked more closely and realized the men were burning railway ties. They must have stolen them. The railway ties made Art think of his father—that and the fumes brought tears to his eyes. The sheer sides of the ravine rose up around him.

There were two men sitting by the firepit—one looked old, the other young. A boy, Art thought, though he wasn't good at guessing ages. They were thin and drawn, their clothes tattered, the old man in a pair of broken-down shoes, the boy barefoot. Neither seemed to notice Art standing there.

Art's captor spoke. "Where are your shoes?"

"They got wet," the boy replied. "I put them out to dry in the sun and they got stole."

"Stolen."

"That's right."

"That was stupid."

The boy gave a small nod and looked back down at the fire.

"How are you going to march to Ottawa now?"

"I guess I ain't."

"Am not."

"That's right."

The old man cleared his throat and tipped his hat back off his face. "Where'd you get that child?" he asked, looking at Art directly.

Art fought the urge to hide behind his captor.

"Picked him up along the way," the man said, and he laughed.

No one else laughed.

"What you gonna do with him?"

"I've got a plan."

"You'll cause trouble with the town," said the old man.

"The good townsfolk will come out here and lynch you," said the boy. "They'll lynch all of us."

"Give them the excuse they been waiting for," said the old man.

Art felt tears slide down his face but he kept his mouth clamped shut.

"What's your plan?" asked the boy.

"You'll have to wait and see."

"Does it involve the girl as well?"

Art and his captor turned around to look. It was Peg. She was making a beeline for them, clutching a stick like a baseball bat. Art wiped his eyes with his fists; he didn't want Peg to see he was afraid. She advanced toward Art's captor swiftly but when she went to take her swing, he lifted the stick clean out of her hands and then broke it over his knee and chucked it onto the fire. Peg put her hands on her hips and looked affronted. The other men hooted with laughter.

"Theodore," said the old man, "you got two of them now."

"What you gonna do with two little kids?" asked the boy. "There'll be trouble. You'll bring trouble down on our heads."

"Shut up," said Mister Theodore. "Shut up, both of you."

He grabbed Peg and Art by an arm each and dragged them over to one of the lean-tos, a perilous-looking structure made of broken-down fruit pallets and canvas. He grabbed a ball of twine off an apple box that served as a table. He then marched them over to a skinny old pine tree, made them sit down on either side of it, and tied them tightly to it with the twine.

"Ah, they're just kids," shouted the boy. "You big bully."

Art leaned his head against the tree. It was not comfortable, but it was not uncomfortable either. They were in the shade and sitting down and, most importantly, they were together. He'd been tied to trees before, more times than he liked to admit, and he'd tied plenty of other kids to trees too, and had taken it in turns to fire Archie's rubber-tipped arrows at them while hooting loudly. But this time was different. He was afraid.

"We found the jungle," Art said.

Peg sighed. "We did."

"It's not like what I expected."

"I need to pee," said Peg.

Art wished Peg hadn't said that. She had a bladder like a camel, at least that's what their mother always said. Art didn't know about camels, but Peg seemed able to hold it for days. The idea that Peg needed to pee made Art want to pee very badly. He tried to focus on being scared instead.

"Do you think they'll eat us?"

"No," said Peg.

"What makes you so sure?"

"They're hobos. They're not cannibals."

"They might be both. Cannibal-hobos. There might be a big pile of bones behind that lean-to." He saw the bones now, plain as day, bleached by the sun, picked clean by hobo-cannibal teeth.

"They're just men who don't have jobs and don't have money, and they're living here before moving on to some-where else."

"How do you know that for sure?"

"That's what Daddy says. They're unemployed." She

pronounced the word confidently. "They're not cannibals. They're marching to Ottawa."

"What's in Ottawa?"

"The Prime Minister. He'll give them jobs."

"What's the—" Art stopped. He could feel Peg's shoulders shaking. He knew she was not laughing. Maybe she was shivering? But she couldn't be cold.

"It'll be okay, Peg," Art said, though it felt odd and unnatural, offering reassurance to Peg-the-brave. "I'll protect you."

He would protect her, and he knew that she would protect him right back. But they were only little kids. Art felt his stomach twist even tighter. They were going to be in such trouble when they got home. Their mother was going to be hopping mad. If they didn't get eaten first.

Art closed his eyes.

Time passed slowly. After what felt like hours, a tiny chipmunk, neat black stripes down its back and tail, came out from beneath a rock in front of Art, followed closely by his friend. Art held his breath and hoped they'd come closer but they scrambled off into the brush. A while later, Mister Theodore announced he was off for a bath; he issued stern instructions to Glen, the boy, to keep watch on the captives. Art wondered where the bath was, picturing a green pool beneath a tree, maybe a secret swimming hole that you could only get to by climbing down a vine. Once he was gone, Glen and the old man began conferring.

"We should let them go. They'll run on home and no one will be any the wiser," said Glen.

"Well," said the old man slowly. He wore a pair of spectacles that were the same as Art's father's, small oval frames, delicate and fragile-looking, except one of the old man's lenses was held together with a homemade bandage of sorts. Art's father treated his own spectacles with care; they had their own special case and he only wore them when he absolutely had to, preferring to navigate most of his life half-blind. He hated to see any kind of careless breakage or waste and he was good at fixing things. Dad would be sorry to see the old man's specs.

"You know how Theodore gets."

Glen nodded, looking worried.

"Besides, he's got a plan. Might be on to something."

"I sure hope so," Glen said.

After a while—Art had no idea how long they'd all been sitting there—Glen untied them one at a time so they could relieve themselves. He took Peg up the ravine first and when he came back for Art he said, "I'm a very fast runner so don't even try." While Art did his business Glen turned away. Afterward, he tousled Art's hair in a friendly manner and said, "All right, boy?"

Art nodded and felt emboldened to ask a question: "How old are you?"

"Me? Fifteen. I'm fifteen years old."

"Why aren't you at home with your mother?"

"What? When I can live a life of freedom on the road?"

Glen said, and he waved his hand in the direction of the ravine, at the mess and the stink. He barked a bitter laugh and said, "No more questions."

After Glen tied them securely to the tree once again, he admired their tin cups as he filled them with water.

"If you let us go you can have one," Peg said.

Art was horrified. Those tin cups belonged to their father.

"No," Glen said, shaking his head. "You keep 'em."

Mister Theodore returned, his wet hair dripping.

"How's the water? Any warmer?" asked the old man as he fussed over a wooden barrel that they'd set up, protected from the elements by its own little lean-to.

Mister Theodore shook his head. "That lake is as cold today as it was when there was snow on the ground."

There was no secret green pool; they took their "baths" in the lake.

"We need more sugar," the old man announced. He gave the barrel a stir, and filled the mugs the two men held out to him.

Mister Theodore drank his down and gave an enormous shudder. "Gut-rot," he said.

"Hooch needs sugar," said the old man.

"Plenty of sugar in cherries," Mister Theodore replied.

The old man scowled as he refilled the mugs. "Needs sugar," he repeated.

Mister Theodore emptied his mug again, held it out for more, and then drank that down just as rapidly. He stumbled as he aimed for a stump, and sat down in the dirt instead.

"Drunk already," said Glen, laughing.

Drunk. Art had never seen a drunken man before.

"Damn cherries," Mister Theodore said to no one in particular. And then, more loudly, "Damn cherries give me the trots."

He wandered over to where Art and Peg were tied.

"You want some of my hooch?" he asked, holding out his mug to Peg.

"I'm eight," said Peg.

Mister Theodore laughed.

"You should try it," he said.

"Leave 'em alone," Glen called over. "Poor kids."

"You want some, boy?" He leaned toward Art.

Art considered. He was awfully thirsty. Mister Theodore handed him the mug. But one sniff of the dark liquid was enough to make Art turn his head away.

"Be a man," Mister Theodore said. He reached for the mug, but before he could grab it, Art took a swig. The liquid burned all the way down into his stomach. Art felt as though his eyes might pop out of his head.

"Atta boy," said Mister Theodore. He grabbed the mug back and finished off its contents. Then he lay down in the dirt beside Peg.

"What's he doing?" Art whispered.

"I ain't doin' nothing," he replied. "It's a free world. I can lie down where I like. I can do what I want. I'm a free man."

After a while, he began to snore. "He's asleep?" Art asked. He wanted to be sure.

"Yes," Peg replied.

The cherry hooch continued to burn in Art's stomach. He'd never felt anything like it.

The shadows in the ravine grew darker. All the men in the jungle seemed to have wandered off or fallen asleep.

Art could hear the train in the distance. His father would be on that train, coming home from working on the track up the line, coming home to his wife and his kids and the house he had built on Woodruff Avenue. Art usually found the sound of the train exciting—'Here it comes!' his brother Eddie would shout, 'Daddy's on it!'—but today it sounded mournful as its chug and whistle echoed back and forth across the lake. He thought about shouting out, thought about asking Peg to shout out at the same time, thought about whether or not they could make enough noise so their father would hear them above the sound of the engine and the wheels and the steam and the brakes. But he knew it was impossible. The train tracks were a long way away, high up above the ravine. And shouting out and not being heard would only make Art feel worse. So he sat in silence, the bark of the tree pricking through his shirt, droplets of pitch hardening in his hair, listening to the train pass by.

They'd be in trouble when they got home. They often stayed out all day but they were expected to be home for supper, they were always home for supper, all four children lined up with their hands and faces clean. Art thought about his mother and her pots and pans and her apron and her newspapers and her magazines and her radio and her doilies. She was famous in the town for reading the newspaper every day. Well, maybe not in the town, but on their street—in their family, at least. Her fingers were often blackened with ink, and she scrubbed them with the potato scourer in the kitchen sink. She always knew what was going on, what the politicians were getting up to down in Victoria, over in Ottawa. She attended the meetings in the town hall where the grown-ups gathered to discuss—well, whatever it was they discussed. Peg showed every sign of being just as interested in that side of things as their mother. Art thought it was a waste of time, and Peg would pinch his arm whenever he said so. His mother loved her radio and her news, but she also loved doilies. She'd tried to learn how to make them, but the fine, slow needlework had infuriated her, it did not suit her nature, so she collected them instead. There were doilies everywhere now, on every surface, on every shelf and side table. Art was not fond of doilies. Whenever he passed by one it would slide to the floor or crumple into a corner, and he'd get the blame.

"You all right, Art?" Peg asked.

They hadn't had much to say to each other while they'd been sitting there against the tree.

"Yes," Art said.

"I'm going to ask Dad again if I can go to work with him."

"He won't let you, Peg, you know that." He wasn't going to take Peg, not when she was ten, not when she was twelve, not when she was fourteen, not ever, on account of her being a girl.

She didn't reply. Neither of them had the energy to fight. Art was glad she didn't argue with him—going to work with his dad one day sometimes felt to Art like the only thing he had to himself, the only thing that was his and his alone.

After what felt like a long while, Art might even have fallen asleep, Peg nudged him with her elbow and whispered, "Those rolls are in my bag." Peg's satchel was on the ground beside her, next to their father's flask and the tin cups. Art thought about those rolls. Their mother had made them this morning—she made a fresh loaf and rolls most mornings, up early before the heat of the day. Art wondered if Mister Theodore had ever had a roll as good as one of these. He'd remember if he had.

Turned out Peg was having the same thought. "We can parlay the rolls for our freedom."

"Okay," said Art, "good idea." Though he wasn't entirely sure what "parlay" meant.

"Mister Theodore!" Peg shouted. "Mister Theodore!"

Art shouted too. "Hey, mister! Hey!"

Their captor roused himself from where he was snoozing and brushed himself off with a yawn. The fire was smouldering.

"You can't keep them tied up there forever, Theodore," said the old man.

Mister Theodore did not reply. He made his way over to the tree. He seemed to have sobered up. Art wished they hadn't woken him after all.

"What do you want?" he said.

"We've got food."

"I know."

At that, the boy and the old man both perked up.

"You've got food?" Glen asked.

"We'll give it to you, in exchange for letting us go," said Peg.

Mister Theodore laughed, as though what Peg had said was silly. Art's stomach rumbled loudly.

"Do it," said Glen.

"What have you got?"

"Two ham rolls."

"Two ham rolls," Glen repeated. "Ham." He closed his eyes.

"We'll have those," Mister Theodore said. "Where'd you get them?"

"Our mum."

"Is there more where they came from?"

"Yes, of course," said Peg. "She bakes every day."

"Except Sunday," Art whispered. He didn't mean to interrupt.

"Except Sunday," Peg said.

"On Sunday she cooks roast dinner after church," Art whispered. He could taste it.

"Roast dinner," said Mister Theodore.

Glen groaned.

"Here's the problem," Mister Theodore continued. "If you give me those ham rolls and I let you go, that's it. That's the end of it."

"Okay," said Peg.

"We won't tell nobody," Art promised.

"Anyone," said Mister Theodore. "If you tell anyone, I'll come after you. I swear."

Art shook his head. He'd take the secret to his grave. He would never ever tell anybody.

"But that's not enough." Mister Theodore paced back and forth in front of them. "Where do you live?"

Art recited their address rapidly. It had taken him ages to memorize it but now he knew it perfectly. Saying the address out loud made him feel better. But after he spoke, Peg elbowed him sharply. Why'd she elbow him? Then it dawned on him. He felt sick. Why was he so stupid? He could have given Mister Theodore an address on the far side of town, or a made-up address even.

"Here's what I want you to do," Mister Theodore said. He went over to the lean-to and disappeared inside, emerging a few moments later holding a pail with a wooden lid. "This is mine," he said.

Peg nodded.

"You're going to take this pail home with you. And every morning—and I mean every morning, including Sundays—before you head out to do whatever it is you kids do all day, you're going to put food in it, and you're going to leave it somewhere I can find it, somewhere no one else will notice."

Art piped up. "By the back steps." There was usually an old bucket or two sitting there anyway, no one would notice one extra.

"Is that a good spot?" Mister Theodore asked Peg.

Peg considered. "Yes. But men come round the back door all the time asking for food, asking for money. You'll have to be quick about it, so that our mum doesn't see you."

"She sees pretty much everything," Art added.

"No cherries," said Glen.

"No frigging cherries," said the old man.

"If there's food in the bucket every day, I'll leave you alone." Mister Theodore towered over them. He seemed as tall as the tree they were tied to. "Miss a day, and I'll come after you. I'll find you, regardless of where you're hiding. I'll pull you out of your beds and drag you both through town and I swear"—he looked up at the sky—"I swear, I'll drag you back to this camp and I'll cook you and eat you. Do you hear me?"

"Yes, sir," said Peg.

Art nodded so hard he thought his head might fall off. He felt the cherry hooch rise up into the back of his mouth.

"Okay. Glen," Mister Theodore called the boy over. "Untie them."

Glen undid the knot and pulled loose the twine that bound them to the tree. Art scrambled to his feet. Pins and needles. He gave a great shudder like a dog shaking off water. Peg got up more slowly. Moving with deliberation, she undid the buckle on the satchel, pulled out the two rolls in their grease-proof paper and unwrapped them carefully.

"I have to take the paper home or Mum will be annoyed with me," she said.

"You take the paper home then."

Art could smell the bread and the meat. So could the men. Peg took a few steps toward Mister Theodore with a roll in each hand. He made a little bow and took them from her.

Peg turned to look at Art, and they were off, Art directly behind her, scrambling up the path as quickly as their feet would take them.

Once they were out of the ravine, Art realized the sun hadn't gone down and it was still very warm. The ravine was a cool, dark place, not sun-baked and bone-dry like the open hillside. It wasn't as late as Art had worried it might be. There were still people on the beach, and when they ran through town the stores were all shut but there were folks still about, and Art wanted to shout "I'm alive, I'm alive," but he didn't. As they came up the street toward their house they slowed down. Art could see his big sister Tilly and his mother in the back yard taking the washing down from the clothesline while they kept an eye on Eddie, who was always eager to pillage Dad's tomatoes. And Dad was there too, kneeling to one side of the back steps, the side nearest the street, the very place where they had said they would leave the pail, and he was painting one of the boards there, a board that Art had helped him replace the weekend before. It was a summer evening like any other summer evening—the family had had dinner, and now they were finishing their chores, and soon everyone would go to bed.

Most nights when Art was in bed, he listened to his mother and his father talking in low voices on the other side of the wall, as his sisters and brother slept nearby, and he felt safe and loved and happy. His mother worked hard to keep the family fed and clothed. His father had a good job on the railway, he left for work on Monday and came home on Friday, and he was lucky to have kept his job during this Depression, this Great Depression that seemed to be a remarkable thing to the grown-ups and had been going on for as long as Art could remember.

He thought now about the men in the ravine. They didn't have jobs. They didn't have a house with a roof and beds and a kitchen table. He thought about Glen, who was only a boy really, despite living in the jungle like a grown-up. Art wondered how long he had been on the road and he wondered if he missed his family. He thought about Mister Theodore, lying down on the rough dirt in his lean-to, pulling his coat over himself because he didn't have a blanket. Or a throw that his mother had knitted. Or a pillow that had been his since he was a baby. Going to sleep hungry after drinking that cherry hooch, and them all so sick of cherries. Art found it difficult to imagine being sick of cherries but then again, maybe. If you had nothing else to eat.

That first night, getting food into Mister Theodore's pail was a straightforward task. Their mum had put on a show of being annoyed that they were home late, but really she was cheery because their father was home, and their supper was waiting for them on covered plates in the pantry. Their father sat with them at the table as they ate, listening to the radio.

Art watched as Peg pretended to put things in her mouth, dropping them into the napkin on her lap instead. Art was so hungry that the idea of giving up a single mouthful of food was almost too much to bear, but he knew it had to be done. Slowly, carefully, he knocked a piece of potato, a mouthful of meat pie, off the edge of his plate. It took all his effort not to pick it back up and eat it, especially the pie. His mother made delicious pie.

Their father left them to clear up after they'd finished. Art followed Peg into the kitchen. They placed their napkins in the bottom of the pail, which Peg had positioned on the floor of the pantry behind the flour bin, and then Peg closed the pail's wooden lid.

The next morning, sticking closely to the plan they'd agreed upon, Art fetched the pail from the pantry and carried it gingerly outside as though it was made of the most precious china. He looked along the street but there was no sign of Mister Theodore. That feeling he'd had yesterday—of being watched—was back again. He placed the pail down beside the back steps and ran into the house.

After that, they developed a routine: they'd save what they could from their plates at dinner and transfer it into the pail in the pantry when they were clearing up. They became expert at scavenging bits from their meals, and between them they usually salvaged a couple of pieces of potato or carrot and a small chunk of pie or meat. Art was more than happy not to eat his vegetables. And if they took small enough quantities of extras—one slice of bread, a sliver of butter—their mother wouldn't notice anything was missing. Sometimes he'd take a bit of something off Eddie's plate when no one was looking—Eddie usually dropped half his supper on the floor anyway. Art saw that Peg had begun to take a kind of pride in it, the amount she could manage to get into the pail each day, and so he doubled his own efforts.

It became Art's job to install the pail by the back steps before everyone else in the house was properly awake, and to tuck it away in the pantry before dinnertime. The pail was always returned, always empty, the napkin neatly folded. The last thing Art wanted was to see Mister Theodore again, so he made himself scarce during the daytime, in the house or off up the street, or down at the lake with Archie.

As the summer holidays passed, their task began to get more difficult. The soup kitchen at the church was feeding yet more vagrants, and Art's mother was volunteering there every other day. She contributed as much as she could to the effort and this meant there was less food on their own table. Art was hungry, he was always hungry. All the swimming, all the running and playing, and the chores—sweeping the steps, front and back; helping his dad fence in the big vegetable patch "to prevent temptation," as his father said, and "stop the poor devils from taking what is not theirs to take"—meant he was hungrier than ever by suppertime. He struggled to stop himself from eating everything on his plate, but the sharp looks Peg gave him and the memory of Mister Theodore's warning kept Art in line. Mister Theodore would hunt them down and drag them away.

Art's feeling of being watched did not go away. And the urge to tell his parents grew. Art wanted to tell them so badly he sometimes lay awake half the night thinking about confessing everything right down to the last detail. But he wasn't about to let Peg know that. Admitting he wanted to tell their parents would make him look cowardly, and besides, if he did tell, they'd put a stop to it, and then Mister Theodore would be out for vengeance. Instead, he tried to persuade Peg to let him tell Tilly. Tilly was the eldest, thirteen and practically a grown-up already—at least that was how she acted most of the time, bossing them around as though she was their third parent. But Tilly could also be a good ally: she'd help you out if you got in a fix and he knew she could keep a secret. When Art threw a newspaper at Peg and hit the teapot instead, breaking off the handle, Tilly hadn't told on him but had showed him how to glue it back in place so it looked almost as good as new, and she'd held his hand when he confessed to their mother and presented the mended teapot to her. He thought Tilly might help them now. Besides, if they had a third person involved, he reasoned, they could eat a bit more themselves.

"No," Peg said. "She'll tell on us. There's no way Tilly will go along with stealing food."

Stealing. That's what they were doing. Hearing the word made Art feel unwell.

"But she can help us get food," Art said.

"No, Art," said Peg, "she'll tell and we'll be in such trouble you won't believe it. Can't you keep a secret?"

"'Course I can."

"Then don't you dare tell Tilly."

In the end, Art agreed. But the hard nut in his belly grew a little bigger every day.

It was an August afternoon—the peaches and plums well and truly ripe and the apricots almost finished—and Art was coming home from the beach with Archie. They'd been at the lake all afternoon; the town had installed a big square floating dock where the water got really deep, and everyone was busy showing off their running dives. Archie and Art had gotten fed up with waiting their turns and instead were concentrating their efforts on seeing who could swim under the dock fastest. Art found this contest terrifying. Even though the dock was brand new, below the water line it already looked monstrous, blackened with slime, the pale floats like udders from enormous cows, trailing ropes that wrapped themselves around your legs as you swam by. He couldn't bring himself to look up at the dock as he swam, but he didn't want to look down into the black depths of the lake either, for fear of what might rise up out of the murk. But he couldn't close his eyes and swim blind as then there was no telling what might happen. None of this was fun, but it did mean that he usually won the race, propelled by terror.

Archie and Art walked up Main Street together, their bare feet summer-hard on the burning sidewalk, to Archie's father's store where they chose what they reckoned to be the two finest peaches. Mr. Portman took great pride in creating a display of local produce every morning, which Art's mother said was "overpriced and for tourists only" because no one from the Okanagan bought fruit from the grocery store when they could buy direct from the orchards instead. Archie was an only child and he walked around the store as though he owned it, which made Art laugh. They took their peaches to Mr. Portman, who was busy with a customer, and he nodded them on their way.

Out the back door and into the alley. There, a man was bent low, rummaging through a pile of empty wooden boxes. He straightened up and looked at the boys. It was Mister Theodore.

Art felt all the air leave his lungs. He couldn't move. Archie looked at Art, and looked at the man, and looked back at Art as if to say, Should I go get my dad? Art shook his head. He'd face up to this on his own.

"Well, hello there."

Mister Theodore's voice was all too familiar; Art heard it nearly every night in his dreams. He couldn't move and now he couldn't speak, either. Mister Theodore's hair and beard were longer than before and his skin had turned a funny kind of yellow. He looked even more frightening.

Mister Theodore held out his hand.

Art looked down at the peach he was holding. It might have been the most beautiful peach he had ever seen. He could tell by the way the flesh felt beneath the soft furry skin that it was perfectly ripe. He could smell it; he could almost taste it.

He walked the few steps that separated him from Mister Theodore and handed him the peach. Mister Theodore inspected it, then slipped it into his pocket.

"Don't think this means you're done with the pail for today."

Art shook his head again. He felt sweat trickling down his back.

"And remember—I'll come after you. I'll come after your family." Mister Theodore took a step toward Art. "I'll snatch that sister of yours off the street."

Art gave a small nod.

"Go on now. Skedaddle."

At that, Art took off up the alley. He ran all the way to Woodruff Avenue and didn't slow down 'til he reached the prickly brown grass in the front of his house.

Archie slid to a stop beside him. "Here," he said. He'd managed to hang onto his peach all the way home and he handed it to Art now.

"I don't know why he took it off me," Art said. "They don't even like fruit anymore."

"Who was that?"

Art's stomach lurched. He'd have to explain.

As he told the story, he could hardly believe it himself. The more he talked, going through what had happened step by step, the lighter he began to feel. He was relieved that after such a long time, nearly the whole summer, it was no longer a secret, relieved to share it with his friend.

"Tied to a tree?" Archie's eyes were wide with amazement.

"Yup. For a whole day. We thought we'd never get away."

"Jeez."

Art realized for the first time that what had happened—the whole thing, including today—was quite a story.

"They menaced Peg something awful."

Archie looked horrified. "Peg?"

Art nodded. "I had to protect her. They threatened to beat me something awful as well." Art couldn't help improving on the tale as he told it and Archie's responses were rewarding.

"Beat you!"

"They made me drink alcohol."

"They did?"

"I got drunk." Art remembered the cherry hooch burning in his stomach.

Archie laughed gleefully and Art felt happy.

"What did he mean about the pail?"

"The pail?" All the pleasure Art felt departed. He didn't want to talk about the pail.

"Yeah—the man said not to forget about the pail."

"We have to put food in the pail," he said, his voice low. "We agreed so they would let us go. Every night we put food in the pail. And I leave it out by the back steps every morning."

Archie was frowning now. "You steal food for them?"

Art nodded, his gut twisting. Steal. Was he a thief?

"We have to, Arch," he said. "Either that or—", he smacked his fist into his palm. The thwack of flesh on flesh made him feel sick.

"And Peg goes along with it?"

Art nodded. "She's good at getting the food. Better than me."

Archie looked worried. "But that's not . . ." his voice trailed off.

Now Art felt even less triumphant.

"If you tell a soul, a single soul, Archie . . ." Art said.

Archie held up his hands. "They'd have to torture me."

Art looked at his friend. Could he trust him?

"Even if they tied me to a tree and let ants run up my legs," Archie said.

"Even if they covered you in honey and fed you to the wasps?"

Archie nodded solemnly.

He'd have to trust him. He had no choice. Art chucked the peach pit into the lilac bush, put his sticky hands around Archie's sweaty, freckly neck and commenced wrestling.

Peg knew already that Art had something to tell her. She had a sixth sense that way. When he took the food he'd collected at supper—most of his meal, he'd felt too worried to eat—to the pantry, she was there waiting.

"Let's go outside," she said.

"Peg and Art, you're on dishes," their mother called out.

"Going outside to cool off first," Peg replied.

Art followed her down the back steps dutifully. They walked to the end of the yard, beyond their dad's vegetable patch. Art inhaled the peppery smell of the tomato plants.

They'd eaten later than usual and the sun was going down. The town hissed lightly around them as the houses and the streets and the trees cooled down.

Peg lay on the brown grass and looked up at the sky. "When I'm big," she said, "I'm going to live in a house with a view of the lake."

"When I'm big," Art said, "I'm going to live in lots of different places. When the dishes are all dirty, instead of washing them, I'm going to move to another house."

Peg laughed.

"When the laundry piles up, I'll leave. When the bed needs changing, I'll say my good-byes."

"You can come and stay with me when you get tired of travelling."

Art nodded. "I'm going to have a good job and I'll make a lot of money. I'll bring you presents, Peg."

"Candy."

"Doilies."

Peg gave him a shove. "No doilies."

Side by side, they looked up at the moon that was appearing in the pale evening sky.

"I saw him," Art said.

Peg took a breath. "I knew it. Where?"

"In the alley behind Mr. Portman's store. He made me give him the peach I was going to eat."

"Did he try to grab you?"

"No. Archie was there with me. I had to tell Archie, Peg. I told him everything. I told him about the pail."

Peg sighed.

"He can keep a secret."

"I hope so," she replied, her voice heavy.

"We have to keep leaving the pail out."

"I know," Peg said.

"Mister Theodore will come after us. He said he'd grab you in the street."

"I know," she repeated.

The problem with Archie knowing what had happened in the jungle was that he wanted to talk about it at every opportunity. Whenever they were on their own, he drilled Art for details, asking the same questions over and over again. What was the jungle like, how many hobos were there, what were they doing? What was in the pail today? He was amazed that Art had kept it a secret, and was in awe of himself even for his role as bystander when they'd met the wicked Mister Theodore. At first, Art was horrified; he'd spilled the secret, and now he had to keep on spilling it over and over again. But Archie found the whole thing completely thrilling, as though Art had had the most enormous adventure, and truth be told, Art began to enjoy it. He liked the fact that he was in possession of this incredible adventure story, that it was something that had happened to him and nobody else—well, Peg, of course, but she hardly counted now, her role got smaller and smaller with each retelling.

Archie was dying to tell all the other kids what Art had

done. Everyone talked about the hobos all the time—they'd become part of the landscape, something the town had to reckon with, had to continue to reckon with, day after day, week after week—and Art could see that Archie was bursting with the story, that whenever anyone mentioned the words "hobo" or "vagrant" it was all he could do to stop himself from shouting it out. But, to his credit, he didn't spill the beans.

It all went wrong the day after the church picnic. The picnic took place on the Sunday before Labour Day every year—an afternoon of games and races, with bunting in the trees and blankets on the grass. It was the only day of the year Art's father would go swimming; he'd march into the lake, his ancient wool trunks held up by a fraying rope belt, carrying the baby Eddie under one arm, the rest of his children hanging onto him, screaming. At the end of the afternoon, the congregation always put together a potluck feast, potato salad and corn on the cob and cold meats, and some of the women would take the opportunity to show off by producing extra-special treats, lemon pie with sky-high golden meringue on top, cherry pie so dripping with juice you'd have to run back into the lake to wash after you'd finished eating it. It was Art's third-favourite day of the year, he liked it almost as much as Christmas and his birthday. The big kids played with the little kids, even Jimmy Tucker from across the street who was Tilly's age and would never even talk to Art normally. They all took turns piggybacking Eddie across the sand and into the lake,

Eddie hollering "giddy-up!" at the top of his voice. Everyone was happy. This year was no different, despite the concerns some townsfolk had voiced about the wisdom of holding an event on a public beach when there were so many unemployed men in the area. There had been talk of moving the picnic to the Stevenses' big spread, but no one apart from the Stevenses cared for that idea. So they went ahead with it anyway. The games were played, the races run, Art and Peg dunked their father under the water. Once night began to fall, they trailed home after their parents, and fell into their beds asleep already.

Peg nudged Art awake the next morning.

"Art," she was saying. "Art. Listen to me. Art."

He raised himself up on one elbow and looked at her. She was crouching down beside him so as not to wake the baby—who wasn't really a baby any longer, he was nearly three years old and already knew most of his numbers.

"We forgot to put the food in the pail," she said.

Art woke up all the way.

"Oh, no."

"We need to do it," she said. "But Mum's already awake—I can hear her."

Art tried to think. "The cellar," he said. "I'll get something out of the cellar and I'll put it in the bucket. That way we don't have to take anything out of the kitchen."

"I'll stand guard."

"I'll climb out the window."

"What?" said Peg.

"I'll climb out. Watch."

The children's bedroom, which had been built onto the back of the house as a kind of afterthought, as though their parents hadn't planned on having any children but then found themselves with four, had a high, long window that opened onto the back porch. Peg was forever hatching plans that involved climbing out of the window at night—her bed was closest to it—but she'd never actually done it. Art often lay in bed wondering if it could be done, if they could leave the house without their parents knowing.

He climbed up onto Peg's bunk. But there was an obstacle: the window had a screen on it. Of course—his father had installed bug screens on all the windows that past spring; Art had helped him. They could be undone and removed, but only from outside. He'd have to go through the kitchen.

"What are you doing, Art?" It was Tilly. Art looked down at her and wished again that they had told her about the jungle. She'd know what to do. He could see that everyone was awake now, including baby Eddie, who gave Art a big smile and said, "Art on Peg's bed," and waved.

"There's a big spider," Peg said. "He's getting rid of it for me."

A big spider, Art thought—where? And since when was Peg afraid of spiders? Then he realized. "Got it," he said. "Let's take it outside." He gave Peg a nod.

He climbed down and they headed out together. He'd been cupping his hands as though he had really caught a spider, and he wiped them against his legs now with a shudder. Their mum was in the kitchen.

"If she comes through," Peg whispered, "I'll stamp my foot hard, three times."

Outside the house, the air was cool and clear. Art slipped down the back stairs as quietly as possible and found the pail in its usual place. He picked it up and went round to the root cellar door. His dad had been talking about putting a lock on the cellar on account of all the men wandering through town, but he hadn't got round to it yet. Art used the pail to prop open the door and crouched down to enter the space.

Art hated the cellar. It was dark and smelled of mice and dirt and mouldering apples and potatoes, like somewhere a witch would lock up naughty children. He wondered what he could reach without actually going in. He grabbed the first jar he touched and brought it out to the daylight. Peaches. No good. He'd have to go in.

He crawled inside, his eyes adjusting slowly to the dimness. This summer's stock of canned fruit lined the shelves. Art's parents canned everything—apricots and plums and cherries and peaches—but he also spotted a row of beans, and soon there'd be at least two rows of tomatoes. He turned around, careful not to knock anything over. There were definitely spiders in here—he should catch one and put it in Peg's bed. Maybe not. He grabbed a small jar of strawberry jam, like a glass full of rubies, and scrambled out of the cellar, closing the door behind him.

They'd never put a jar of jam in the pail before, but it would have to do. Art wondered if his mother would notice. There was a good chance she kept a tally of the canned goods in one of her notebooks, alongside her shopping lists and notes about the town meetings and clippings from the newspaper. But they'd have to take that chance.

He shut the wooden lid and made his way around the back steps, placing the pail in its proper place, relieved to have accomplished his task. He straightened up and turned to head back inside, only to see his father coming round the side of the house with his watering can.

"What are you up to, lad?" he asked.

His father. Art had forgotten he had the day off.

Peg stepped through the back door onto the porch. "Sorry," she mouthed.

He knew they were thinking the same thing: they might be able to steal food, but they couldn't lie to their father. Art's eyes started to prick and before he could stop himself, he was crying.

"Come here," his father said softly, and Art threw his arms around him and buried his face in his shirt.

Peg plonked herself down heavily on the back steps and put her face in her hands. "I'm sorry, Daddy," she said.

"I'm sorry too," Art added. His father drew him over to the steps and sat down. Peg and Art leaned into him on either side. To his horror, Art realized that Peg was crying too. She never cried. She hadn't cried when they'd been kidnapped, had she? You could twist her arm while stomping on her foot and she wouldn't cry.

"Come on now," their father said. "Tell me everything."

—

After breakfast, Tilly was instructed to take Eddie down to the lake while Art and Peg stayed behind. Seated at the kitchen table while his parents stood opposite, Art confessed once again.

"I did it," he said, "I did it," and he was too overwhelmed to say any more.

Peg was calm now, she'd stopped crying almost as soon as she started, and she answered their parents' questions for the both of them, her voice even while Art snuffled and choked. She tried to take the blame for it all. She said she should have known better—she was a whole year older than Art, she should have been watching out for him. They'd both been told to stay away from the hobos and she should have behaved more responsibly.

"You should have run straight home instead of chasing after Art and this Mister Theodore person," said their mother.

"But I couldn't leave him there by himself!" Peg said, growing indignant. "He had Art over his shoulder!"

Shame engulfed him—he was ashamed of stealing, and ashamed of being caught, ashamed at how long it had gone on for, and ashamed that they went looking for the jungle in the first place. And now ashamed that he was allowing Peg to shoulder the blame when he knew it had really been his idea, his fault.

Art's parents had remained calm until Peg described how they'd been tied to a tree all day. At that, Art's father slammed his fist on the table, making the cutlery jump and giving Art such a scare that he started to cry again.

"Did they—" his father paused. He was looking at Peg. "—go near you?"

Art wondered what his father meant. Of course they went near them. But Peg shook her head vehemently.

"Are you sure?" he asked, and he looked at Art.

"No, Daddy," Peg said. "No."

Fat tears ran down Art's cheeks and onto his shirt. He knew they were in terrible trouble. He couldn't imagine what his parents would do. They never hit their children—it was a point of pride in the household, there was to be no violence—but Art was sure they'd make an exception this time. They were going to be spanked, but that was only the beginning of their woes. Mister Theodore would find out they had told, and he would come after them, and take them back to the jungle where he would kill them and eat them. He would take the whole family prisoner this time, Art and Peg and their parents, along with Tilly and even baby Eddie. Art and Peg had broken their promise to Mister Theodore, and those men were hungry.

"You stole from your own family," Art's father said. He sounded very sad. "You took food off our plates."

Now Peg was crying again. Twice in one day.

"Off you go now," their father said.

Art wasn't sure what he meant.

"Go on. Go find Tilly down at the lake."

"Aren't we—" Peg said, "—aren't you . . ."

"Your mother and I need to discuss this. Go on."

Art slid off his chair and followed Peg out the back door. He felt heavy, as though he was dragging his crimes along behind him, *bump bump bump*. His eyes were tired from crying. Peg was walking with her head bowed. They lugged themselves down to the lake where Art went straight into the water. If he just kept walking, would the water rise up around him and close over his head? Maybe he could walk along the bottom of the lake and find the Ogopogo, the ancient monster who lived there, and fight the monster and kill it and the town would proclaim him a hero. Art wanted to be a hero. He didn't want to be a bad boy.

The week passed quietly. Art's father left for work the next day, and his mother didn't say anything about how they were to be punished—in fact, she acted as though nothing unusual had happened. At supper she'd decreed that none of the children were to go beyond the limits of the town when they were out playing, but she'd said nothing more.

"Why would anyone want to do that?" Tilly had piped up, looking at Art and Peg pointedly. She knew the new rule wasn't aimed at her.

They stopped putting food out for Mister Theodore. Their mother had removed the pail from outside, which worried Art to no end because it was Mister Theodore's pail and his mother didn't seem to understand that. But Art didn't say a word, and neither did Peg. He knew they were both too frightened and ashamed to raise the subject with their mother again.

Sometimes Art could almost convince himself the whole

thing had never happened. But his mother had left the offending jar of strawberry jam on the kitchen counter, and every time Art walked past it he felt sick all over again. Art and Peg stuck close to home, too nervous to stray far, both avoiding the spot where they used to leave the pail just in case Mister Theodore showed up. Peg became mother's best helper and took to wearing an apron; she spent her days sweating over the hot stove in the hot afternoon, making yet more jam. Art hung around the front yard trying to lure his friends to play with him as they walked past on their way to the lake. Archie stopped by to show Art his new puppy, Geronimo, but the tiny German shepherd had other plans and was straining to get away.

"We got found out," Art said.

"I heard," Archie replied. "Something's gonna happen."

"What do you mean?"

"I don't know. The grown-ups—they're planning something. I heard your mother talking to mine. The dads as well. Discussing." Archie gave Art a wave as the dog pulled him away.

What could the grown-ups be planning? Why hadn't Art's parents punished him? Was the whole town involved in deciding how he should be punished? Would he go to jail?

Art was possessed by an awful sense of doom. He wondered what Mister Theodore was doing. He was probably in the jungle with Glen and the old man, sitting by the fire, roasting a rat, and drawing up plans to punish Art and Peg for breaking their promise. Probably sharpening his knives. At night Art lay awake, listening, hoping he would hear the hobos coming so he and Peg could hide before they arrived.

The days dragged by, each feeling longer than the last, the late-summer heat stifling. School was set to start the following week and, for once, Art was looking forward to it. He figured school was a safe place to be. Mister Theodore wouldn't dare come there and risk the wrath of the principal.

On Friday afternoon Art sat on the front steps of the house, waiting for his father to come home. When Dad appeared at the end of the street, Art had to stop himself from shouting with relief. The children greeted him with their usual tumult but Art clung onto him the longest, breathing in his railway smell, and when his father hoisted him up onto his shoulders—"Lord, Art, when did you get so heavy?"—he felt the happiest he had all week.

They ate dinner early—their mother always cooked a special meal on Fridays—and everyone praised Peg because she had made the pastry for the pie.

"My tomboy!" said their father. "A cook!"

And Peg's smile was so big Art thought her face might burst and he wanted to kick her, even though the pie was delicious.

There was a music program they listened to on Friday evenings, and everyone took up their usual places in the front room, Art on the floor nearest to the radio. They listened to the music, and their mother sang along from time to time. Tilly had her nose in a book, as always, and Art's father read the newspaper, while the rest of them played cards. Eddie sat on their mother's lap while they played; he had finally been persuaded that whispering the numbers on her cards was not a good idea. Art kept losing; he couldn't concentrate. Normally he was a bad loser, prone to kicking his opponents in their shins under the table, but not tonight.

They'd only played a couple of hands when Art's father stood up, took down his summer hat from its hook, and said he had to go see somebody and that he wanted Art to accompany him.

"Who are you going to see?" Peg asked. She gave Art a look, though he wasn't sure what it meant.

"None of your beeswax," their father replied, and he gave their mother a kiss on the cheek.

Art walked down the street beside his father, too afraid to ask where they were going. It was still light out, and the evening air was as soft as the piece of velvet that Peg had been using for her doll's bed and that Eddie had recently claimed for himself. They were joined by Archie Portman's father from across the way; he was carrying a shovel, the same shovel, Art was sure, that he had used to kill the snake and then the dog last summer. As they walked through town, other men emerged from their houses as though they'd received some kind of secret signal. Jimmy Tucker's father came round the side of his house holding a rake and George Campbell's father joined them carrying an axe. They nodded at each other grimly.

"What's that for, Robert?" Art's father asked.

"You never know when you might need to chop something down," Mr. Campbell replied.

Art thought his father would tell Mr. Campbell to leave the axe behind, but he did not.

By the time they got to the edge of the town there were more than twenty men in the party—Art the only boy. More shovels and spades had appeared as well as two more axes. Art knew where they were headed now. He figured they'd want him to show the way, but it turned out that they'd known all along where the jungle was and Art felt foolish for having thought that he and Peg had been the first and only people from town to find it.

The group paused for a moment by the old railway cottages. The whole town was quiet, as though the very streets and buildings knew something was going to happen. Art thought there'd be a speech—grown-ups loved making speeches—and the outing seemed to call for one. Instead, Mr. Portman leaned over and ruffled Art's hair.

"How you doing, son?" he asked.

"Fine, thank you, Mr. Portman."

"We have to protect the women, Art. It's all very well, you boys roaming the hills—but taking a little girl captive? No," he shook his head. "It's got out of hand."

Art's father put an arm around him and gave his shoulders a squeeze. Art looked up at him. "What's going to happen?" he asked, his voice low so no one else would hear. His father did not reply.

Instead of climbing up through the orchard and along the bench the men picked their way along the stony lakeshore. It didn't take long for them to reach the place where the ravine cut up through the hillside; when Art and Peg had made their journey it had felt epic, like they'd been hiking for half the day, but along the lake the trek only took fifteen minutes or so. They began to climb up into the ravine. Art wished he were brave enough to lead the way, but he hung back behind his father instead, so close he had to be careful not to nip Dad's heels.

The jungle looked empty. Art was relieved: they'd gotten wind of this visit and had left already, Mister Theodore, Glen and the old man without a name. When they reached the first firepit, the men came to a stop. There was no fire in the pit, just cold white ashes. The hooch barrel wasn't there either. Art tugged on his father's hand and whispered, "No one here." Again his father didn't answer him. Instead, he took a deep breath.

"Time to leave, boys," he said, loudly. "Time to move on."

Mr. Portman began to dismantle one of the old lean-tos, throwing the wood into the firepit.

"Come on, lads," Mr. Campbell shouted. "We don't want anyone to get hurt."

"We're going to burn it out," Mr. Tucker shouted, and he unscrewed the lid of a bottle and poured something into the firepit—at first Art thought it was water, until the sharp smell of gasoline reached him. Mr. Tucker lit a match and the pile caught fire with a *whoosh*.

At that, there was movement. Further up the ravine, the sound of scrabbling, and then he saw them, the hobos emerging from their makeshift tents and their falling-down lean-tos. At first Art thought they were going to advance down the hill as a group, but they were busy gathering together their paltry belongings.

"If you see the man who grabbed you and Peg, point him out," Art's father said, and the other fathers looked at Art and nodded, as though to reassure him.

Mr. Tucker began to move up the hill with his bottle of gasoline, setting fires in every firepit that dotted the ravine. The other men from town followed him, breaking down the lean-tos and throwing them onto the fires as they went. Mr. Campbell pulled the siding off one hut and a half-dressed man tumbled out clutching his worn old boots in one hand—"Let me get my kit!" he shouted, "at least let me get my kit."

Gradually, the jungle emptied out. As Art's father and his friends worked their way uphill, dismantling the camp, the men who had lived there climbed higher, up out of the ravine, fanning out across the hill in all directions. Art kept close to his father. They reached the tree where he and Peg had spent that long, hot afternoon tied together. Art turned away from it quickly, he didn't want anyone to know he'd been tied up here. He nearly shrieked when he realized that the old man was sitting on his perch nearby, watching the proceedings as though they had nothing to do with him. He gave Art a nod.

Glen was nowhere to be seen and Art hoped Mister Theodore was gone too. But then he emerged from his tumbledown lean-to, looking taller and thinner and even more yellowish than before. Art began to back away slowly. He thought if he held his breath and moved as quietly as possible, he might not be noticed.

Mister Theodore was holding a framed photograph of a woman. "Where's that newspaper?" he asked the old man, as though there was no one else present, no great group of townsmen destroying his home. The old man pulled the paper up from behind the log he was sitting on and passed it to Mister Theodore, who wrapped it carefully around the picture.

"Hello, boy," he said and he looked at Art sideways.

Art didn't reply. His heart was pounding.

Art's father arrived at his side. "Is that the man?" his father asked.

Mister Theodore turned and looked directly at Art. Art's stomach clenched.

"No," said Art with a croak. He shook his head adamantly. "No."

"Come on," Mister Theodore said to the old man. "Let's go find Glen." And they made their way up the side of the ravine, Mister Theodore leading, the old man, hunched over and wheezing, climbing slowly behind him. Art thought then that these men were like a little family and as he watched them retreat, he found himself wondering what it would be like to go with them, to hit the road, jump on a train, hitch a ride in the back of a truck. What would it be like to leave his parents and his sisters and Eddie—his town, his house—behind? And he felt a weird kind of longing for this life so different from his own, even though he knew he could never bear to leave.

Mr. Campbell took his axe to Mister Theodore's lean-to. Soon the jungle would be no more.

On the way back into town, the evening light fading fast, Art trailed behind the grown-ups. They were excited by what had happened, their voices loud as they told and retold what they had seen, what they had done, how the vagrants had run away with their tails between their legs. Art couldn't help feeling a bit sad. He was sorry for the men who had lost their homes, even though he knew what Mister Theodore had done—had made him and Peg do—was wrong. And he was disappointed that the jungle no longer existed; no matter how scared he'd been all summer, part of him had still liked knowing it was there. Now it was gone, and the pact to fill the pail was finished as well. He wondered where the hobos were heading—where would they bed down for the night?

Once back at the railway cottages, the grown-ups paused to confer. Art wandered across the tracks and pocketed a few flat skipping stones. When he turned back it was as though the men had puffed themselves up somehow, turned from a straggly crew of fathers into a unit of soldiers, with their shovels and their pickaxes at the ready once again. They moved ahead purposefully. "Where're we going?" Art asked. No one answered.

Because the hobos had occupied the railway roundhouse, the trains now had to be shunted onto the sidings when they weren't in use. One of the passenger carriages, sitting on its own in a siding, had recently been broken into. Art could see that his father and the townsmen were headed for it. He hung back without being told to do so. He didn't like this expedition. He wanted to ask his dad if he could take himself home, but he couldn't spot him in the gang.

The men surrounded the lone carriage on all sides. Mr. Portman hammered on the window with his shovel. He began to shout "Out! Out! Out!" and everyone joined in with the chant. Art could see people inside the carriage, looking through the windows like passengers on their way to Midway. One man had made his bed on the roof; he was sitting up there dressed in what looked like pyjamas, clutching a satchel. Art wondered for a moment if his father and the others were going to set fire to the carriage, like they had the jungle. The shouting and banging grew louder and louder until a hobo opened the rear door of the carriage and stepped out onto its little platform. Despite the warmth of the evening, he was wearing a coat buttoned all the way up to his neck. He raised his arms and Art saw he was holding a shotgun. He pointed his weapon into the crowd below him. The men took a collective step backward and fell silent.

There was a pause. A long pause.

The man fired. Everyone screamed and Art started screaming too, rooted to the spot as everyone else ran here and
there, tripping and stumbling and jostling each other. Someone bumped into Art so hard he almost lost his footing. Then
he heard a voice shout, "Get him!" and several men surged
toward the man with the gun, climbing up onto the carriage.
Just when Art thought he might faint from terror, his father
emerged from the crowd. He grabbed hold of Art and hugged
him close and put his hand across his eyes, but without thinking Art pulled the hand away. That was when he saw a man
lying on the ground beside the railway carriage, his face a
bloody mess, no longer recognizable, the top of his head blown
clear away, a shovel on the ground beside him. Mr. Portman's
shovel.

Where was Mr. Portman? Art looked around at the crowd
that was now settling into silence, staring down at the body.
Where was Archie's dad?

And then Art realized. The man lying on the ground in an
ever-widening pool of blood was wearing Mr. Portman's jacket.

Without a word passing between them, Art and his father
turned away. Art's father took hold of his hand and they
made their way toward home, walking quickly, the commo-
tion at the roundhouse fading from earshot, neither of them
able to speak.

Art went straight to his room and climbed into bed. Every
time he closed his eyes, he heard the bang of the gun, that
deafening metallic bang. He flinched and shrank beneath his
sheet. *Bang*. He felt like he'd never be able to sleep again.

His parents were in the next room, talking. He listened to their voices, their words indistinct. After a while, Art heard his father get up and go out the front door, into the dark street. *Bang.* He turned over to face the wall and tried his best not to cry.

Later, Peg climbed into his bed. They used to sleep together when they were small, before their father built the bunks, before Eddie was born, and her body was as familiar to him as his own. She handed him her hankie.

"What happened?" she whispered.

He didn't want to tell her that the jungle was gone. He didn't want to tell her about Mr. Portman lying dead in the dirt on the ground by the roundhouse. He dried his eyes and blew his nose on Peg's hankie. And then he whispered the words into the hot heavy darkness of the night.

Peg was frustrated that Art had been allowed to go and she hadn't, as though things might have gone better if she had. Maybe they would have—maybe Mr. Portman would still be alive. But she hadn't been there with him. She hadn't smelled the fires burning, she hadn't watched the men scrambling to gather their possessions, she hadn't seen Mr. Portman die. A small piece of him felt glad. Maybe he had protected her for once. Art was the one who'd witnessed it, and this was now his burden, his story, not hers.

When Art went into the kitchen the next morning his father was already awake and dressed in his best—his only—suit.

"I'll go down to the police station, see what's needed," he said to their mother, who was making a meat pie.

"They'll need to eat," she said. "She won't feel like cooking."

Art realized she was talking about Archie and his mum—that it was the day after, and Archie's father was still dead, he really was dead and gone.

It was too hot to hang around the house, so as soon as they finished their chores Art and Peg headed off. They walked past the Portman house and Art was almost too afraid to look at it, but when he did, all he saw was Archie's puppy asleep in the shade on the porch, his leash tied to the banister.

Peg stopped at the edge of the beach, where the melting asphalt met the burning sand.

"Art. Look."

He turned to where she was pointing and there, beyond the town, above the dark cut of the ravine, was a thin column of black smoke. A narrow column rising steadily, spreading its pall over the valley.

They stood and stared, neither of them speaking.

Just then, Jimmy Tucker ran past, clipping Art's head sharply with one hand. "Race you!" Art took a breath and chased after him, Peg close on his heels.

Jimmy plunged into the lake toward the floating dock. Art swam hard but Peg overtook him—she was the faster swimmer. Halfway to the dock Art was overwhelmed by tiredness. He abandoned the race and turned over to float on his back. A thin skin of black smoke coated the sky.

He heard Peg shout, "I won!" She was standing on the dock waving her arms above her head in victory. Jimmy climbed up the ladder behind her, dove straight back into the water and swam over to where Art was floating.

"They burnt them out in revenge," Jimmy said.

"What?"

"Mr. Portman got shot and then the men went out there last night—my dad, your dad too I think—and burnt the jungle down." Jimmy looked across the water toward the ravine. "I didn't even know it was there. The hobos got the hell out. The town is safe now."

Art wasn't sure what to say. Normally nothing would have stopped him from informing Jimmy that he had it all wrong and that Art had, in fact, been with the grown-ups last night and had seen everything, and as well as all that, he had spent a whole day and part of a night in the jungle, and he knew some of the hobos personally, Mister Theodore and Glen and the old man, and it didn't seem like such a bad life, camping out in the ravine, beholden to no one, free. But he remembered how hungry the hobos had looked, how hunger came off them in waves. And then he remembered Archie's father lying on the ground, blood and bone and dirt where he should have had a face.

Art rolled over in the water, onto his front, careful not to look down at whatever was below the surface. Out here the water was black and deep.

—

Mr. Portman's funeral took place a few days later. August had turned into September but the weather had grown even hotter, as though the summer was trying to prevent the fall from ever arriving. Art was wearing his Sunday best, the whole family was in their Sunday best, even Eddie. Art's father had lent Art one of his black hats, which his mother lined with newspaper so it would fit his head. They walked to the church as a unit, Art's parents and Tilly laden with food for after the service. Art had not seen Archie all week—according to his parents Archie had not left the house since it happened, and the thought of seeing his friend again made him feel nauseated. In fact, he'd been sick that morning, coughing up his guts into a pan, and he'd had a wan hope that this would mean he could stay behind. But no. His mother had helped him get up, given him a glass of water, washed his face with a cool cloth and wiped his limbs as well. She was silent and solemn and tender, and Art felt as though it was his body that was being prepared for burial.

They dropped the food off in the hall and made their way into the church. People nodded in greeting, the adults murmuring in low voices, the organist already playing what Art's father called "her dismal tunes." The church was crowded and they squeezed into a pew next to the Tucker family, Art squashed between his mother and Mrs. Tucker, Eddie on his mother's lap, squirming, Peg up at the other end with Tilly. He'd never been to a funeral and so far it didn't seem too different from a particularly well-attended Sunday service.

Mrs. Tucker turned to Art with a strange, harsh smile. "I

hear this is all down to you and your mischief, Arthur Lunn," she said, still smiling.

Art felt as though he was going to be sick once again. He wanted to sink down into the pew and vanish.

"Well, Eileen, I think you'll find that vagrant is to blame." Art's mother's voice rose above the low hum of the congregation. People turned to look.

At that moment the organist paused and the congregation fell silent, and Art felt sure that God was about to strike him dead. But everyone's attention, including that of his mother and Mrs. Tucker, had moved away from him to the church doors behind them. Art craned his neck to see what was happening. The organist started up again, this time louder and even more dismally, and everyone stood as the minister led the way up the aisle. Six men were carrying what Art realized must be Mr. Portman's coffin. Art was startled to see his father bringing up the rear, the coffin resting on his shoulder. The bearers were followed by Mrs. Portman, dressed in black with a veil covering her face, and Archie, who looked even paler and skinnier than usual in a brand-new store-bought black suit. Art's friend stared resolutely at his shiny black shoes as he made his way up the aisle, all the way to the front pew where he took his seat beside his mother.

Art had never been able to understand the minister, with his Scottish accent and his old-fashioned way of speaking, and today he didn't even try. *I hear this is all down to you and your mischief.* Mrs.Tucker's words banged back and forth inside his head. Was that what everyone thought?

And then it dawned on Art: what had happened *was* his fault. He should never have gone to the jungle, he should never have convinced Peg it was a good idea. Because of him, they'd been kidnapped, they'd had to steal the food, the men of the town had burnt the camp down and the hobos had been made to leave. Because of his . . . *mischief*, Archie's father was dead.

Art lowered his head. He could hear someone nearby sobbing, breath catching in their throat as they tried to keep quiet, and it dawned on him that it was Peg. His mother put her arm around him and tried to pull him closer, but he resisted. He didn't deserve her embrace.

1942: Rose

IT WAS ROSE'S BIRTHDAY on Saturday but Art knew there was no chance he'd be able to see her that day, which was why he'd made this plan. An hour—a bit longer if he was lucky— at Tilly's place, him and Rose. Alone. The very thought made him feel victorious and unworthy at the same time.

Most days it was Peg who had the run of Tilly's after school. It was infuriating how Peg acted like she was special just because she was the only one who had been at the wedding, the only one to have met Duncan Wilson. That didn't give her exclusive rights when it came to Tilly. At least he'd managed to persuade Peg to let him have Tilly's place to himself today. He was surprised by how quickly she'd agreed—he hadn't had to threaten to twist her arm. He'd stopped actually fighting her ages ago, when he realized one day that he was twice her size. Turns out there's no pleasure in fighting your sister once you can win all the time. Besides, Peg's fighting days were over, she was a proper lady now, or at least that's what she wanted people to think. Not someone who roamed the hills looking for hobos. But Art knew better. No matter how seriously she took on the rank of lieutenant to their mother's major general, a love of adventure was buried deep within her. Art knew it, and he could see it in her. Like an itch she wasn't allowed to scratch. And so when he told her his plan—Rose's birthday—she lit up.

Rose was not like other girls. She was graceful and reserved and full of purpose. She had a seriousness to her that Art could tell the other girls found confusing. She didn't decorate her school notebook with hearts and flowers. She didn't flutter her eyes. She didn't talk about wanting to get married and have babies. Her mother was French, from France—as tall and slim and straight-backed as Rose, with the same dark hair—and if you were lucky enough to see them in town running errands together, you might hear them talking to each other in that mysterious language. She was an only child; Rose's father was lining her up to work for him when she finished school, to help run the orchards he owned as though she was his son, and this was another thing that marked her out, along with the athleticism she possessed from working the land. Rose was impatient to leave childish things behind, and Art felt this was something they shared. He wasn't a child, he was a man, even if nobody else seemed to realize it.

But getting to see her was not easy. She lived up the lake, far enough that her father drove her into school every morning and picked her up at the end of every day. Her family didn't come into town much beyond what was necessary; they didn't even belong to a church, though Art knew Rose's mother was Catholic. Unlike everyone else he knew, Rose didn't hang around, she didn't skate in the park in the winter or sunbathe on the floating dock in summer. But once a week, on Tuesdays, Rose stayed in town after school for her piano lesson. This meant that on Tuesdays there was a window of time before the lesson when Rose was free to do as she liked. And lately, that had meant spending time with Art.

Most of the time, they sat together in the grounds of the school, near the big old oak tree by the fence where there was a bench. When it was too cold or wet or snowy, they'd head for the library, but Art tried to avoid that because once they got there they could no longer talk. She wasn't his girlfriend, he'd never had a girlfriend, but she wasn't not his girlfriend either. Art found being near her completely thrilling.

And Rose had agreed to meet him at Tilly's place today. He'd offered it to her as an alternative last week and, to his surprise, she'd said yes. All Art had to do now was wait for her to show up. He had a birthday present for her—Tilly had helped him buy and wrap it. But he hadn't exactly told Tilly that he had invited Rose over. He wasn't sure if Tilly would object—she was as much a romantic as Peg—but he didn't want to risk it. Besides, Tilly would get home from work just after five, and by then Rose would be at her piano lesson.

Art was fifteen. He felt like he'd been fifteen forever, and would remain fifteen for the rest of time. Stuck at school because his parents wouldn't allow him to leave—sometimes literally stuck because the desks were so damn small. Stuck in the town where he'd lived all his life, where everyone knew who he was, not because he was good-looking (which he was, of course) and brave and bold but because of something terrible that had happened when he was seven years old. Seven. A long time ago.

He was a worker, a good worker, and he grabbed every chance to prove it. Long summer days with his father and the bridge-and-tunnel crew, pumping the handcar along the track and through the cut to fetch water, sweat in his eyes, his arms straining, crossing the trestles at full speed, through the tunnels, rushing into the darkness and pumping hard toward the light. And in the winter, on the weekends, odd jobs for the company down at the roundhouse. He was a quick learner with a good memory.

At the Portmans' across the street, he'd taken on much of the work Archie's father used to do around the yard: digging out Mrs. Portman's vegetable bed in spring, mowing the lawn in summer, raking the leaves in fall, shovelling snow all winter long. Mrs. Portman kept the store going strong through the Depression and on into the war, and Archie worked there after school and on weekends. It still looked just as good as when Mr. Portman had been in charge, the summer fruit display as lavish and inviting—for tourists—as before. If anything, the business seemed to have grown busier, as though the town wanted—needed—it to stay open. These days, Mrs. Portman was an angry woman at the best of times, forever shrieking at Archie so the whole street could hear. She'd even shout blue murder at him in the store, though as soon as anyone walked through the door she'd stop, give the long counter a polish with her cloth, and smile. As would Archie. Art found it alarming. He avoided the store. But he made sure that when Archie and his mother came home at the end of the day, they didn't have to worry about the yard work they'd left undone.

Art and Archie. The best of friends. Archie never said he blamed Art for what had happened that day. Except of course he did. He showed it in tiny ways, gestures no one else could see. Last summer he'd jumped off the dock and landed on Art's back with both feet, pushing him deep under water before Art had a chance to take a breath. And just last week Archie had tripped Art as he'd walked past his desk at school; when Art picked himself up, laughing along with everyone, he'd been startled by the look of malice on Archie's freckled face. Best of friends. Always.

Although he liked the work, Art already knew that he didn't want to follow in his father's footsteps. The problem with working on the railway was that while the trains took you away on Monday, at the end of the week they brought you home again. And then the grass needed clipping. And the snow needed shovelling. And it all repeated itself, over and over again. Art wasn't interested in playing at keeping house. He wanted more than that.

No sign of Rose yet. Art got up to look at the clock on the mantelpiece—only five minutes had passed since he'd last checked. He stalked over to the window and stared out at the empty street. And back to Tilly's mantelpiece. Tilly always kept the most recent—almost always brief, often censored—letter from her husband propped up there. "He can't write more for fear of giving something away to the enemy," she'd explained. Today there'd been a letter lying on the mat when Art had come in, pushed under the door by Tilly's landlady, and he'd stepped over it carefully, unwilling to deny his sister the pleasure of spotting it, reaching down to pick it up, her heart soaring.

Art took yet another look at the portrait of Tilly and Duncan Wilson, taken after their wedding ceremony, Tilly in a hat with a little veil and Duncan Wilson in his uniform. Tilly had married a hero, an airman, a lieutenant, who was somewhere *over there*, god knows where, fighting a hero's war. He was like a kind of movie star, a glimmering figment of the family's collective imagination, embodied by his letters, the photograph on the mantelpiece and Tilly's undying love. It *was* romantic, even Art could see that.

The news about Tilly's wedding had also arrived in a letter. That day, Art had come home from school to find Peg and his mother sitting at the kitchen table, his mother clutching a note, the envelope in front of her on the table. He could see that she'd been crying, and this was almost as startling as the news the letter contained. Eddie wasn't home yet—he was up the street somewhere, playing. It was early October but the afternoon sun was still warm enough to make you want to stay outside until it was dark, when a chill would finally roll down off the hills and up from the lake.

His mother had handed him the note. *Getting married next week! . . . he's due to ship out any time now . . . I know it's unlikely any of you will be able to come . . .* The letter was short, but Art could feel his sister's happiness, right there on the page, as though the words themselves were smiling.

"She's forgotten to tell us who she's marrying," his mother said. She blew her nose, tucked her hankie into her sleeve, and smiled valiantly.

"Duncan Wilson," Peg said. "I think it might be him."

Art looked at his sister. How did she know that?

"Who?" their mother asked.

"Duncan Wilson," Peg repeated. "She's mentioned him in her letters to me a few times."

After Tilly had finished high school last year, she'd enrolled in the Sprott Shaw Business College. The decision to send her to Vancouver was met with widespread though largely unspoken disapproval by their neighbours; Mrs. Portman had been among the few to actually say it aloud. "A girl needs her family around her," she said. "Vancouver's no place for a young woman on her own."

Art had felt his mother stiffen at that. They were outside the church, after Sunday service. His father was helping to set out tables in the hall, Tilly had gone off to fetch Eddie from Sunday school, and Peg was in a crowd of her friends over by the gate. Art realized at that moment that his mother didn't like Mrs. Portman. Perhaps, like him, she felt she owed the Portmans a debt, one that no amount of homemade pie and shovelled snow could repay.

"There's a war on, Davina," Art's mother said. "Our young people need to contribute. Women as well as men. We need people with professional skills and qualifications."

"There are other ways—"

"—I don't doubt that," Art's mother interrupted. "But this is the way we've chosen."

Mrs. Portman looked affronted. At that moment, Archie and Peg arrived and they were both laughing at something. Art was always surprised to see how normal Peg was around Archie, how she was able to treat the Portmans like neighbours, nothing more, nothing less.

And, in fact, Tilly was at college in Vancouver for only a couple of weeks before she secured a job in the offices of the rapidly expanding shipyards in North Vancouver. *There's plenty of work*, she'd written, *in the shipyards and the docks, and over at Sea Island as well. Manual labour, of course, but there's a big need for clerical help too, which is why I got lucky.* Tilly worked six shifts a week and continued with her classes in the evenings. It sounded like a tough life, in the big city far away from them all. But her letters home had gradually become more cheerful, until they began to fill up with the friends she had made, the places she'd been—*out dancing 'til late . . . walked home with my friend Lois in the pouring rain . . . learning to roller skate*—and in letters to her younger sister, apparently, a few references to "Lieutenant Wilson," "Duncan Wilson" and, most recently, "Duncan."

"He's in the air force. Lieutenant Wilson," Peg said. "She's known him for a while."

Art's mother looked up at Peg hopefully. "Oh?" she said.

"He sounds nice," Peg added, and she smiled her brightest, most reassuring smile. "She's happy."

The decision was taken to send Peg to the wedding. She'd returned home with the corsage that Duncan Wilson had bought her pressed between the pages of her library book, full of talk of the glass of champagne she'd drunk at the Hotel Vancouver after the simple ceremony and of the city and the ocean and the soldiers, all the soldiers, as though they'd been there for her entertainment and not because there was a war that needed fighting.

The war. It was easy to forget about it. His parents and sisters followed the news carefully, especially now, with Tilly's husband overseas—his mother, with her newspapers and her radio, frustrated at what she considered to be a severe shortage of actual information. Many of the young men from town had gone off to fight but they were older than Art and he hadn't paid them much heed. He had other concerns. Rose, for one.

Art sat down in Tilly's armchair. Maybe Rose wasn't going to come today. Maybe he was kidding himself that a girl like her would want to be more than friends with him. Maybe he'd read the signals all wrong.

And then there it was. A knock on the door—soft, hesitant. He leapt up to answer it. Rose. In all her glory.

"Hello, Art," she said.

He took a deep breath in and pushed it out.

"Hi, Rose," he said, and closed the door behind her. "How are you?"

She smiled. She stepped close to him on tiptoes, took his face in both her hands, and kissed him. On the lips. Art could not have been more surprised. He felt his temperature rise. How could someone's lips be so soft? She moved away.

"I'm all right," she said. She walked into the centre of the room, looking around. "I've never been in a boarding house before."

Art wasn't sure he could speak. He gave himself a shake. "Me neither," said Art, his voice a little too high. He cleared his throat. "At least not before Tilly moved here."

"A place all to herself."

"I'm not sure this was what she expected when she got married."

Rose shook her head gravely.

"Her husband—Duncan Wilson—Lieutenant Wilson—shipped out overseas a couple of days after the wedding. He thought it would be best if Tilly came home for the duration. Safer here than on the coast. But she didn't want to move back home, on account of having to share a bedroom with all of us." Art couldn't believe he had used the word "bedroom" in front of Rose and began to blush. "So she got a job working as a secretary to the notary public, Mr. Hutchison—he doesn't mind employing a married woman because he's known Tilly practically her whole life and, besides, plenty of married women are working now. She moved in here and lets me and Peg visit whenever we like." Art stopped speaking abruptly. His heart was racing.

Rose nodded. "Must be nice."

She was here. She was really here. Now Art was struck dumb. Could he walk right up to her and kiss her, take her face in his hands and kiss her lips like she had kissed his? No, that was out of the question. They should sit. But where? Art looked around the room, trying not to panic. There was a wooden chair by the little table, the armchair with its footstool, and the narrow daybed where Tilly slept. None suitable. Why hadn't he worked this out before?

"Let's sit," Rose said. She walked toward the daybed. Art thought he might swoon. She lifted two cushions off the bed and placed them a few feet apart on the rug. She sat down on one, leaned back against the daybed, and patted the other by way of invitation. Art sat down. Rose crossed her legs neatly, her hand on the floor between the cushions. Art put his hand next to hers, so close they were almost touching.

"Oh," he said, "I forgot," and he raised himself up off the floor so clumsily it was as though his limbs were no longer connected to his body. He fetched Rose's present, sat back down beside her with a thud, and handed it to her without ceremony. "Your birthday."

"Golly!" Rose said. "A present!" Her voice was pitched higher than normal and Art realized she was as nervous as he was.

She took her time opening the small parcel. Layers of tissue paper tied with ribbon. And inside, a pair of pale, silk stockings, folded carefully along their seams, bought with money he'd earned working on the railway. When she saw them, Rose gasped. And she said his name, her voice low and confiding. "Art. How lovely."

But at the sight of the stockings, Art was paralyzed with embarrassment. He'd never bought a present for a girl before. Why on earth had he thought stockings were a good idea? Why had Tilly encouraged him? So . . . adult. So . . . good God. He remembered how they'd felt against his skin in the shop.

Rose lifted the stockings out of the tissue paper and they slipped into her lap like they were made of liquid. She picked one up by the toe and stroked her cheek with it; she reached over and did the same to Art, touching the silk to his face. In that moment he thought he might die. He turned to her hoping that she'd kiss him, and instead found himself looking into her hazel-brown eyes.

"Thank you," she said. She took his hand in hers and then rested her head on his shoulder. Art closed his eyes. It felt so good to be near her. He took a deep breath. Rose. How could a person smell so good?

After a while, she spoke. "I saw Peg on my way over."

"Oh, yeah?" he said. "What was she doing?" If she turns up here, Art thought, I'll kill her.

"She was with Archie," she said. "He was carrying her skates."

Art sighed heavily. "He does that. She says yes because she wants to be polite."

"Why would she say yes if she doesn't want to go skating with him?"

"Because he's Archie Portman." Although, as Art said it, he realized it wasn't true. Peg let Archie carry her skates because she was a nice person and she knew it would make Archie happy. Unlike him, she didn't seem to feel she owed Archie anything.

Rose lifted her head off Art's shoulder. "And?"

Art looked at Rose. This wasn't the first time he'd wondered: was it possible she didn't know? She hadn't been at elementary school with them. Her family had never lived in town. Maybe she hadn't been at Mr. Portman's funeral. Maybe her family hadn't followed every detail of the events as they'd unfolded, nor formed opinions they felt compelled to share in the street. Was it possible that when she looked at Art it wasn't the first thing she saw?

The murderer had been arrested straightaway, shipped out to the courthouse in Vancouver and incarcerated in the BC Pen—the town couldn't get rid of him soon enough. He hadn't resisted; he'd lowered his gun and waited to be taken away, as though he'd killed Mr. Portman in order to get a roof over his head. Art's father said the man had something wrong with him, a screw loose, that he'd been driven crazy by the hobo life: as well as having no work, they'd later learned from the newspaper reports that he'd lost his child to tuberculosis and his wife had left him. "No excuse," Art's father had said, "but I was sorry to hear that story."

Maybe Rose didn't know what had happened. Well, if he was going to get anywhere with her, anywhere beyond an hour together on Tuesdays, he'd have to tell her sometime. It might as well be today.

"Archie Portman lost his dad when he was . . . when we were . . . kids."

"Yes," Rose nodded, "I know his father died."

"It was my fault." A familiar heaviness bore down on Art as he spoke.

"How can that be?" Rose asked.

So he told her. The jungle. The clear-out. And the men— the fathers—all gathered around the carriage the vagrants had occupied, shouting. And Archie's dad.

"He was dead. He died."

And he saw Mr. Portman, dead in the dirt, clear as if it were happening now. He looked down at Rose's hand in his, felt the warm weight of it. The skin on her long fingers was rough from working in the orchards, her nails clipped short.

Rose took a breath. This was it. She would turn away from him now.

"You were just a little kid, Art. You shouldn't have been there."

"I know. It was my idea. I made Peg come with me. We wanted to see the jungle."

"No, no, I don't mean that—you shouldn't have been with those men that night. What were they thinking, taking a little boy with them?"

"I wanted to go."

"Of course you did. But they should have known better."

The thought that he shouldn't have been there had never occurred to Art. Why had his father thought it was a good idea to take him to the jungle that night? Could Art have been spared from seeing—and seeing and seeing over again— Mr. Portman die? But no, he'd needed to be there by the railway carriage. He had to bear witness—it was his fault. It made sense for him to be there on that night. And he had been there, there was no escape from that.

"What an awful thing for a child to see," Rose said. And she turned to him and he turned to her and this time he took her face in his hands and kissed her. Once, twice, and again. And this time the kisses rolled through his entire body; nothing had ever felt so wild and sweet.

The clock on Tilly's mantelpiece struck five. "I've got to go!" Rose exclaimed. "I'm going to be late." She got up off the floor and Art followed. He helped her into her coat and she turned to him. "Thank you for the stockings, Arthur Lunn." She smiled as she put on her hat. "Thank you for a lovely time."

And she was gone.

Art gave himself a shake. He put on his own coat, buttoning it slowly. The stockings on his cheek. Kissing.

He locked the door to Tilly's place. Outside, it was dusk and the air smelled of autumn. Art walked through town, the familiar streets made strange to him. He felt light-headed, light of body, as though he might float up off the ground if he wasn't careful. She'd kissed him. He'd told her the truth, and they'd kissed again. He couldn't believe it. He felt giddy.

He turned into his street. From his post on the porch of the Portman house, Geronimo sat up as Art passed by, making the almost-bark sound he made when he wanted attention. Archie and his mum would be at the store still. Art decided he'd fetch the outdoor brush and sweep the leaves off their footpath. He'd do the front steps as well.

1944: All Hail the Conquering Hero

BY SPRING, MOST OF ART'S FRIENDS had shipped out. They'd enlisted, every single one of the older boys. Even Archie Portman—who was nearly a whole year older than Art despite being in the same class—had signed up back in September, the day he turned eighteen, while Art still rattled around school, under-age. Archie's departure, on the same day as Jimmy Tucker's, had made Art feel lousy; he was off to be a hero while Art was stuck at home with the girls. And to make matters worse, once he was gone Art felt a confusing sense of relief at not having to see Archie every day.

And even more annoyingly, Peg had gone and got married. To Frank, a schoolteacher, a big, soft lummox of a man with a fancy university education. Specs so thick you could start a fire with them. Frank had some kind of problem with his feet that rendered him unfit to fight—though not so unfit he couldn't play tennis. He volunteered for the war effort instead, teaching math to new recruits up in Vernon on the weekends and during school vacations, as though soldiers needed to be able to add and subtract before they were machine-gunned by Jerry.

Art wasn't sure why it made him so damn mad that Peg had gotten married. It was what girls were supposed to do, after all, it was what Peg had always planned to do—she'd caught the marriage bug after she went down to Vancouver for Tilly's wedding. It was to be expected. And it wasn't as though he was all that close to his sister, not anymore, not since she'd been domesticated. But she used to be his ally, his backup, his running mate. They'd once been tied together up against that tree. She wasn't supposed to grow up before he did, even though she was older. She wasn't supposed to leave him behind—why was everyone leaving him behind?—and for a life that was so damn ordinary, too. He liked to pretend Peg had never gotten married, and this wasn't as hard as it might have been because whenever Frank was up at the training camp Peg returned to the bedroom at the back of the house. They'd lie in their beds and see who could be the first to make Eddie laugh so hard and loud their mother would come and tell them off for making a racket.

Art probably should have guessed what would happen when Peg started climbing out the bedroom window last fall. Now he was the one who did all the climbing out that window, except it was mostly to go night swimming by himself because none of the girls from school had figured out how to sneak out, and Rose lived too far up the lake.

Things weren't all that great with Rose. They'd had a brief, blissful phase of meeting at Tilly's place on Tuesday afternoons, but Rose had taken her grade eight piano examination last year and, after that, her lessons had stopped. Her father continued to drive her to and from school, despite the fact that Rose had learned to drive as soon as she was old enough, same as Art. Strict parents were one thing, but Art felt that Rose was unwilling to get away. He would have been happy to drive up the lake to see her, but that wasn't in the cards—he'd never been invited. She'd told Art that her mother wasn't very well, and because of that, she was needed at home. But when Art pressed her, it seemed her mother wasn't physically sick, but unwell in some other, hard to define, way. He didn't know what that meant—only that Rose didn't have time for him.

And yet, when they were together, it couldn't have felt more right. At school, they ate lunch together every day, stealing a kiss under the big tree over by the fence when no one was looking, and walked to and from class when their timetables allowed. But that was it, that was the extent of their courtship, if you could call it that. And there were plenty of girls in town who were more than willing to let Art take them to the movies or out to a party. So that's what he did. He could tell this infuriated Rose, but she was too proud and stubborn to admit it.

Marriage was for idiots, as far as Art could tell. Peg remained the only member of the family to have met Duncan Wilson—the man was still overseas, flying planes. For all intents and purposes he didn't exist and Tilly might as well have been single. But Peg had gotten married, despite their sister's poor example. And Art's friends had signed up and shipped out.

Mrs. Portman had been so proud of Archie, her son heading off to fight for his country. "She's lost her marbles," Art's dad had said at the time, "her only child. She can't really mean she wants him to go." But off he went. And Art had continued to attend school, all day, every day. His parents had a bee in their bonnet about education, the education they themselves hadn't received, and they were determined that their children would be high school graduates, all four of them. Well, Art couldn't see the point.

One sunny morning on his way to school, Art crunched through the icy remains of what everyone hoped was the last snow of the season and, despite the fact that he wouldn't be eighteen for another five months, turned right instead of left at the end of the street and hitched a ride up to Vernon. It felt like everyone else had done it, and Art was not going to be left behind.

The town buzzed with action. As Art walked from where the car dropped him off to the recruiting office he could hear gunfire coming through the pines from somewhere beyond the barracks. *Pop pop pop.*

Bang.

Mr. Portman lying dead on the ground.

Art stopped walking. The colour had drained out of the world. He started to shake.

Art had continued to help out across the street whenever

he could, especially now that Archie was overseas. After he finished the yard work, he'd sit awhile on the Portmans' porch beside Geronimo. Geronimo would put his head in Art's lap and look up at him as though there was no one else in the world he'd rather see and it made Art feel sad somehow. Lonely. "We miss Archie, don't we, buddy," he'd say to the dog as he scratched his head.

Pop pop pop.

An officer walked toward Art, looking sharp in his crisp uniform and tidy moustache. "Enlisting?"

Art nodded, mute.

"Good man," he said emphatically. And he took Art by the shoulder and ushered him into the recruiting office.

While he waited for his papers to arrive, Art kept the fact that he'd enlisted a secret. There was no point in quitting school: if he wanted to quit he'd have to tell the principal he'd joined up, and the principal would tell the teachers, and the math teacher was Frank, and Frank was Peg's husband for Pete's sake, so Frank would definitely tell Peg and now that she was all married and proper Peg could no longer be relied upon to keep a secret. So she would tell their parents and that would give them time to figure out how to prevent him from going, which wouldn't be difficult, given he was under-age. So he kept attending school.

A few weeks later, Art got home to find both his parents seated at the table—formal, tense, as though they'd been waiting for him for hours. There was an unopened envelope propped up against the teapot. Art realized it must be for him. At that same moment, Peg arrived through the back door, calling out hello. Her cheery bluster vanished as she came through from the kitchen and saw the looks on their parents' faces. She remained standing at the threshold of the room as though she couldn't decide whether to come in or flee. Art gave her a look, willing her to come in and sit down, but she resisted.

Art picked up the envelope. It bore his full name: Arthur Harvey Lunn. He'd never received such an official-looking letter before. His heart pounding, his parents and sister watching closely, he tried to open the envelope with care, but he fumbled, his hands too big, his fingers stiff. He pulled out the letter and read it quickly, once, twice. The date he was to present himself was there, in bold type. He knew today's date, but he walked over to the Royal Bank calendar hanging on the wall to confirm it. Three days' time. It occurred to him that he had no idea how long he'd be gone.

"Well," he said, still standing by the calendar, "as you can see, I have some news. I'll be shipping out."

His father sat with his arms folded tightly across his chest as though to prevent an outburst. His face was an alarming shade of red. Art could see he was angry, but, more than that, he could see he was disappointed. He hadn't expected his father to be disappointed in him. He'd known they wouldn't be thrilled that he'd be leaving school without graduating—that was why he'd kept it a secret. But his parents followed the news about the war closely—the battles, the "zombies" guarding the coast from the Japs, the politics of conscription; at the end of the day, Art thought signing up had to be what they'd expected, despite the fact he'd gone and done it a bit earlier than anticipated.

"Maybe I'll be sent to England," Art said in the hope of lightening the mood. He looked at his mother. "If I get leave I could visit your sister." He had an aunt in the Fens, where his parents came from.

His mother sighed.

"We came to Canada to get away from bloody war," his father spluttered.

Art knew his parents had emigrated right after the Great War; they'd travelled by ship and then train across Canada. It was why they'd waited so long to start a family.

"You shouldn't have lied, Art," his mother said.

"I didn't lie," Art said. He'd licked his finger and smudged his date of birth on the form, but he wasn't about to tell them that.

"I have half a mind to bloody well head up to Vernon myself and inform them," his father said.

Art's father never swore. And now he'd sworn twice.

As though he couldn't bear any more talk, his father stood up from the table abruptly, sending his chair flying. "I'm not having it." He went to the front door, jammed his hat on his head, and left.

This was not how Art had expected the news to be received. He turned to his mother.

"Your father lost two brothers in the war," she said. "The last war."

"What?" Art's stomach lurched.

"Both his brothers."

Art's parents didn't talk about the past, they didn't tell stories about their childhoods, about their lives before they came to Canada. Art had only a vague outline: when his father was a kid he'd worked on a farm where they grew sugar beets. He'd fought in the war but never discussed it. But two brothers lost in the war? He swallowed hard.

"Well, no one told me that. And besides," Art blundered on, "that was then and this is now."

"He was hoping the war would end before you . . ." his mother's voice trailed off.

Peg piped up, her tone as chipper as she could muster. "You'll see the world, Art!" She crossed the room and stood beside him, smiling.

Art was grateful. He put his arm around his sister and gave her a squeeze. "Thanks for taking time away from your tennis to come and visit."

Peg landed a soft punch on his arm. "You enlisted because Frank's a better player than you."

"Frank is not a better player than me."

"He is."

"It's that music you play. Too loud. Throws me off my game." Frank would park his car—he had a car!—beside the courts, open the windows, and turn up the radio as loud as it would go. Often the tennis matches would devolve into dancing, the music attracting other youngsters from the neighbourhood. Peg and her doubles partner Nancy would make Art dance too—and Eddie, who was nearly thirteen and should have known better, would run around and around like an over-excited puppy. Art hated dancing almost as much as he hated tennis. Well, that wasn't true. It wasn't true at all. He loved dancing—what could be better than swinging around with a girl on your arm?—and he liked tennis well enough. It was doing these things with Frank that was annoying. The man was a schoolteacher with bad eyesight, bad feet, bad teeth, and he hadn't been allowed to enlist, though he looked well enough to Art.

And with that, the discussion was over. Art's mother went into the kitchen to start supper. Art, released, slipped out the front door of the house, Peg behind him.

"Haven't you got a home to go to?" he said.

"Why'd you do it?" she asked.

The list of local men who were never coming home from the front was already long. He knew most of them, everyone did. It was hard to believe they were gone; part of him believed that once the war ended they'd all be resurrected.

"You expect me to sit here like a bump on a log? It's a man's job, being a soldier."

"You're not a man. You're still a boy."

He stepped away from his sister, his arms spread wide, as though in submission. "The men have all gone, Peg. Just girls left now. Girls."

A dig at Frank. Peg let it wash over her. Then she stalked off the front porch and made her way down the street.

Art's father came home as Art was laying the table for supper. He took off his boots and hung his hat on its hook. He looked at Art and said, "Will you ask your mother to make me a cup of tea?" Then he sat in his chair and picked up the newspaper.

Art went to school the next day as though nothing had happened, as though he wasn't about to ship out overseas. He asked Rose to meet him at lunch under the tree over by the fence, the same spot where they met most days.

Rose. She had her life all worked out. She was still planning on working for her father full time once she finished high school. She'd already started taking correspondence courses in the evenings—double-entry bookkeeping, whatever that might be—preparing to run the orchards herself one day.

She slipped her hand into his and he kissed her. He breathed her in. She always smelled great.

"I've got some news," he said.

She pushed up against him, one hand on his hip, the other on his shoulder as though she thought they should dance. Sometimes when he was near her he thought he might faint.

"I've joined up," he said. "I'm heading out on Monday."

"You what?" Rose said.

He reached out to draw her near again but she pulled away.

"Enlisted," she said, her voice dull. "To go to war."

He nodded and gave her his biggest smile.

"You're stupider than I thought you were, Arthur Lunn."

Once again, this was not the reaction he'd been expecting.

"But, I—"

"—Don't think I'm going to wait for you like some idiot girl who thinks her fellow is going to return from war the all-conquering hero."

"The all-conquering—what?" Art felt heat rise through his body. He *had* expected Rose to vow to wait for him, even if he wasn't entirely sure of where he stood with her. He'd also hoped that maybe she'd find a way to spend a bit more time with him—maybe even this afternoon—before he went away.

"You're doing it because you want people to think you're a big man."

"I'm not!"

"You are! You joined up just to say I told you so." Rose's face had pinked up and Art could see her eyes were brimming.

"I didn't—I—"

"—Well, why did you do it, then?"

"Well, I . . ." Art paused. "To stop people thinking of me . . ." He couldn't say it out loud—to stop people thinking of him as the boy whose idiocy led to that terrible night in the town, the jungle on fire, and Archie Portman's father dead. Art was haunted by this judgment almost as intensely as he was haunted by the sight of Mr. Portman's smashed-in head. He enlisted to stop seeing it, stop feeling it. Plus every other young man he knew had signed up, so why shouldn't he? There was nothing extraordinary about it—it was as inevitable as day turning into night.

Rose spoke again. "Off you go, then." She waved a hand.

"Rose," he said. "Rose, come on."

As she turned away he could see that she was trying, and failing, to stop herself from crying. He heard her breath catch in her throat. At least there was that.

When Art signed up he thought he'd be whisked off to the front. He'd pictured himself roaming the hills of Europe on the lookout for Germans, not unlike how he once roamed the hills above the lake watching out for snakes, except he'd be wearing a smart uniform and carrying a rifle with a great long bayonet. He couldn't have been more wrong. Foolish. He'd been whisked off, all right, but to Ontario: Camp Borden, Simcoe County. Weeks and weeks and weeks of training, and most of his duties resembled those of a glorified janitor. And southern Ontario? Flat. Nothing to see for miles. And big, loud mosquitoes. And horseflies that took chunks out of any flesh you were ignorant enough to expose. And that sandy dirt underfoot, in your socks, in your hair, clagging up the back of your throat. There were no bayonets, though he did get to know his way around a rifle. It took him a while to get used to the sound of gunfire, to not flinch and shrink, to stop seeing Mr. Portman whenever he heard a gun go off.

He spent his downtime with his fellow recruits, teeing up and hitting golf balls on the shooting range with a 4-iron one of the officers had donated to the cause. He liked the camp, with its neat rows of barracks, its mess hall, shower block, laundry. He even liked the rules and regulations and the way that getting them right, knowing what to do and when, made him feel part of something big.

When he was finally deployed, Art's regiment was stationed near a small seaside town on the Adriatic that had been destroyed by an epic battle the previous Christmas. The sky was the bluest blue, the sea was turquoise and sparkling. The town was ancient, a warren of narrow stone streets coiling around a hilltop castle that looked out over the deep-water port. The battle had left the whole place devastated: bombed, blasted, entire streets reduced to rubble, as though the castle itself had rolled down the hillside, crushing everything in its path. The allied troops had created mouseholes through the buildings, punching through the walls between houses so they could move across town without being seen by the occupying Germans. What hadn't been blown up was now falling down.

By the time Art arrived, the Germans were gone, and the fighting was moving steadily north through Italy. At the camp, only a handful of German prisoners were left. Art's unit was in a kind of gentle limbo, patrolling, recovering, waiting to be deployed, servicing the troops as they were moved north. Though he was keen to fight, once he heard the stories the rest of the men had to tell, the Loyal Eddies and his own regiment, the Seaforths, he began to change his mind. Most of his unit had fought in the long battle for the town, not just hand-to-hand combat but room by room, house by house, so close you could smell the enemy's breath. They'd lost hundreds of soldiers, too many dead for Art to comprehend.

Everyone knew that Art had signed up when he was under-age, and even though he'd turned eighteen during those long months he'd spent in Ontario training, the men in his unit liked to think of him as permanently seventeen. They conspired to terrify him with their stories of carnage and combat in streets too ruined and death-clogged for army rescue vehicles to access, while at the same time keeping him out of harm's way. He was called "Artie," whereas everyone else was known by rank and surname. "You're a fine specimen of a lad, Artie," Lieutenant Langstrom—who was from a farm in southern Alberta—liked to say. "You'll make some girl a lovely husband one day." Then he'd tousle Art's hair or give him a hug and, instead of feeling mocked, Art felt a profound sense of relief.

Art found himself thinking about the hobo, Mister Theodore. Maybe the truth was he'd signed up in order to prove that no one could make him do anything against his will again, that he was a man who could fend for himself. The camp reminded him of the jungle with its smell of firepits and cooking and sweat, but a jungle that, this time, belonged to him. If Mister Theodore turned up now, Art would see him off, show him who was who.

Some of the soldiers were in bad shape. His first night in the camp he'd fallen into a dead sleep at lights out but had been woken at two a.m. by the sound of screaming. He bolted upright and grabbed his boots, like he'd been trained to do. Langstrom, in the next cot, spoke out through the dark, "Don't worry, Artie. It's just Milsom."

"Milsom?" Art said. Was that some kind of training manoeuvre he'd forgotten?

"Lieutenant Milsom. He does this most nights. He's just . . . dreaming."

"Dreaming."

"You get used to it. It's like—" he paused, "it's like those church bells forever ringing in town. You get used to those as well."

Art put his boots down and lay back on his cot. Milsom kept up the racket. Sometimes he sounded like a baby hollering for his mother, sometimes like a cat, or a coyote, sometimes like nothing Art had ever heard before. There were other voices, murmuring—a door slammed, and someone shouted "Shut the fuck up, Milsom!" and someone else laughed. But in his room no one laughed. They lay there, eyes open, listening.

Art had been in the camp for a number of weeks when news filtered through that a unit, moving up from the south, had arrived at the camp to bed down for a few days. Art was in the mess mashing potatoes; the cook had secured a pallet of fresh spuds from god knows where, and since then they'd been eating potatoes every which way: potato fritters, French fries, scalloped potatoes, hash browns, roasted potatoes, and a dish the cook had invented called Potatoes Jubilee which consisted of all the leftover bits of potato fried with canned bully beef. Luckily Art loved spuds. He went out the back door of the mess to fetch another sack.

"Well, hello there."

Art froze. A familiar voice. For the briefest moment he found himself thinking: Mister Theodore?

He swung round.

But it was Archie. Archie Portman, in the flesh. Archie! About a foot taller and, if possible, even skinnier than he'd been before.

"Man oh man," Archie said, "it's about time!" and he gave Art such a great manly squeeze that Art almost stopped himself from thinking that Archie was just about the last person he wanted to see.

Here was the one person in the whole of the Canadian army who really knew who he was, who knew everything there was to know about him.

Archie Portman. Here. In Italy.

That night before curfew, Art and Archie sat out together, sharing a cigarette, the moonlight striking bright on the water, lighting up the coastline.

"They're moving us all north, but they're trying to hide it from the Krauts," Archie said.

"Is that right?"

Archie nodded. "That's the sum total of my knowledge."

Nobody told Art anything, he just followed orders.

"Geronimo is a good dog," Art said. He wasn't sure what'd made him think of the dog, apart from the fact that he missed him.

Archie barked a laugh. "Geronimo. Good boy." He paused. He turned to look at Art. "I heard Peg got married."

That's right, Art thought, you were always keen on her. "Frank Turner. The new schoolteacher. From Burnaby," he added. "Came to town and swept Peg off her feet." Art thought of Peg's wedding the previous winter, the lavish display in the church. The day had been unseasonably warm and the lake had shimmered in the afternoon light, the beach clear. The wedding party was large, no one seemed to know how or why it had got so grand; perhaps because it was the first proper wedding in the family, a chance to make up for Tilly's non-event, her soldier husband Duncan Wilson perpetually overseas.

Mrs. Portman had declined the invitation. "Doesn't seem right," she'd said to Art's mother at church one Sunday, "a big wedding when our boys are overseas fighting."

Art's mother had smiled and looked away.

"Damn," said Archie, shaking his head. "Peg. Married."

Art laughed and gave Archie a shove. "Don't worry. By the time we get home, all the girls will be so relieved to see us we'll have to beg them to leave us be."

He thought about Rose. He thought about Rose most days. He received letters from home regularly, from his mother, Tilly and Peg, even Eddie took it upon himself to send Art compilations of his favourite jokes from time to time. But not from Rose; letter-writing was not her kind of thing. Rose. She'd like the army, Art thought. She loved hard work and routine; if she'd been a man she'd be one of those soldiers who think it's all a lark, a grand adventure, with polished boots and sharp bed-corners and falling into formation. And, when required, she'd be heroic. He had thought he'd be one of those men as well but he knew now he was not. He'd spent enough time sitting in the back of an army transport, with hardly room to breathe and too much time to think, to convince himself of that. And he had not had an opportunity to prove otherwise.

Art had thought Archie would move out with the rest of his unit, "north," wherever that was, but that hadn't happened. Instead, Art, Archie and their crew had become a make-do bomb disposal unit; they were moving through the town systematically clearing unexploded shells and mortar along the way, declaring some buildings safe and many more fit for demolition only. You had to be careful where you tread. They worked in pairs, that was the rule, Art and Archie often together now, everyone assuming "the Okanagan boys" would work best side by side. Archie appeared to be more than happy to work alongside Art—he'd been overseas for nearly a year longer than Art and seemed to want nothing more than to spend time with a friend from home. Art was sure Archie had his own battle stories, but like the other soldiers he didn't talk about them and for that Art was grateful.

According to Langstrom, a surprising number of townspeople had remained during the battle, and now the rest of the locals were beginning to return from wherever it was they'd been hiding. One day, Art and Archie were working in a building where an unexploded bomb had been cleared away the previous week—Archie with his probe, which was in fact a glorified stick, cautiously making his way across what was left of the ground floor, Art shovelling a path behind him—when Art looked out through the glassless window and saw a young woman dressed in a smart hat and matching coat across the street. She was standing in front of a building that pretty much no longer existed, a heap of rubble between two walls. She was carrying two suitcases and Art watched as she lowered them slowly to a patch of ground Art had cleared earlier in the week. After a few minutes she took off her hat. A few minutes later, she took off her coat, folding it carefully. Art thought he'd better go speak to her before she disrobed entirely.

"I'm just going to see if I can help this lady," he said.

Archie grunted a reply, concentrating.

As Art emerged onto the street, the woman spun round as though frightened. Art held up his hands. He'd left his gun propped up inside the house next to Archie's; no one worried much about the Germans anymore. He'd also taken off his jacket and rolled up his sleeves. He thought he'd better speak to her, to show his good intentions, but his Italian remained limited. *"Ciao,"* he said, leaving off the *"bella"* his comrades had told him to use on the ladies whenever possible. "Don't worry. We're clearing up here. We'll be gone soon." In his experience Italians didn't speak English but it was all he had.

He was standing beside her now. She was a bit older than he'd thought, elegant and dark-eyed. He hadn't really had much to do with the locals; they were all around, of course, trying to pull their lives and their town back together. She stared at him now, silent.

"Is this your house?" he asked, turning to look at the ruin. "*Casa?*"

"Yes," she replied in English. "My house, my shop, everything."

"You had a shop?" Art said. "What kind of a shop?"

"Dressmaker."

"Dressmaker," replied Art. He thought of Peg and Tilly and his mother, their endless mending and sewing. "That's a great trade."

Her glossy black hair was done up in a simple twist. She had on a pale pink silk blouse and a pale blue skirt that matched the coat and hat she had taken off earlier. She looked like she should be in a movie with Barbara Stanwyck, holding onto the rail of a gorgeous ship, drinking champagne.

"You are a child," she said.

Art laughed. "Well," he said, "not really."

She smiled. "Canadian?"

Art nodded. He'd gotten used to the way Italians said the word, slowly, as if it required thought.

"What are you doing here? Why not fighting?"

"We've only just met and you want me to leave?" Art said, but she didn't get his joke. "Anyway, I'm too young for all that, you said it yourself."

She turned away. She took a few steps toward what would have been the entrance to her shop and kicked at the rubble, her fine shoes immediately covered in heavy dust.

"There's no point," Art said. "Look at it. Besides, you need to be careful. Unexploded bombs." He brought his hands together and apart and made the noise of a small explosion.

She laughed. Then she looked up, at the clear blue sky that would once have been blocked by her shop—maybe she'd had living quarters up there, with a kitchen and a sitting room and a bedroom. "The door," she said. "The door is here." She pointed at the ground.

A cellar. She must mean the door to a cellar. Art volunteered to fetch his shovel. He brought Archie and his probe along for good measure.

It didn't take them long to clear the door. The heavy metal plate was battered but had held fast. Art turned around to see where she'd gone—she was sitting on one of her suitcases. In her hand, she held a large key.

"What's your name?"

"Arthur Lunn. This here is Archie Portman. And you?"

"Signora Lavelli."

Signora, Art thought. *Mrs.*

She handed him the key.

Winter winds returned to the Adriatic, as though the spring weather had been a tease; some days it was warm by lunchtime, but mostly it was cold and grey which made the town feel grim. Rain came in and conditions in the camp worsened as the army's attention focused north.

"Fucking mud," Archie said one day, "it might be the thing I hate most about Europe."

"There's no mud back home," Art replied. They were overseeing a gang of prisoners who were digging a new latrine. The Germans were cheerful, if a little slow-moving, now that they'd figured out they weren't about to be executed.

"At home everything is brand new and clean and shining," Langstrom added, his voice grim.

After supper, Art got ready, a shower and a shave, combing his hair in a piece of mirror he had salvaged in town. Langstrom was lying on his cot reading a girlie magazine that he'd already read a hundred times at least.

"Card game?"

Art shook his head. "I've got a date."

Langstrom smiled. Soldiers weren't supposed to fraternize with the local population but everyone knew about Art's signora.

"Archie will be disappointed."

"Archie's a grown man."

"You're lucky to have a friend from back home."

Art did not reply.

Art moved through the town quickly. The place was coming back to life, more people were returning, moving back into their ruined houses, reopening their ruined businesses, taking back their ruined lives. Art didn't really understand it—if this was his town, he'd move on. He'd go to Canada. When he'd said this the other day, Langstrom had laughed. "All most people want is to be home with their families, in the place where their families have always been."

Today Art was a bit later than usual, and he worried she'd be gone. But when he lifted the cellar door, he could smell her perfume. He lowered the heavy cover over his head; he knew his way down the stone steps in the dark now. At the bottom, he pulled the candle from his bag and struck a match against the rough stone wall. The cellar lit up with warm yellow candlelight.

It was a small room, more of a crawl space than a cellar, carved into the stone hillside beneath where her shop had once stood. It reminded Art of the root cellar under his house back home, except without the enormous spiders. Everywhere he looked there was colour, bolt after bolt, stack upon stack. The richest reds, the deepest blues, the brightest emerald greens; in damask, tweed, taffeta, velvet, chiffon, lace, seersucker, and fine cottons; in patterns, prints, embroidery; in shimmering lamé and delicate cloth so fine it was almost transparent.

She was asleep. Up at the back of the space, on a broad shelf he had helped her clear, she had made a bed with multiple layers of flannelette and towelling. His boots were muddy, and he cursed himself for not having taken them off the minute he'd reached the bottom of the steps. He removed them now, and then his clothes—he didn't have any underwear on, he'd fallen behind on his laundry—and then folded them all as neatly as he could; he was still no good at regulation army folding.

She was lying beneath a piece of red silk. The cool air made him shiver a little and he eased himself beside her. The silk fell against his skin and he thought of Rose. Rose and the silk stockings he'd given her for her birthday one year. Rose and how far away from her he was now.

He closed his eyes. He was tired. He would rest here beside Signora Lavelli.

But she was awake. She put her hand on his . . . he still wasn't sure what to call it. When she first saw it she'd asked again how old he was, and he'd lied, as always, he lied so often now it came naturally. "Twenty-one," he said. He felt wounded when she laughed. But then he'd seen her face and her look of longing. And now, she put her hand there, and he didn't need to wonder what she wanted, it was always very clear what she wanted, and even though the ceiling was low and they had to be careful not to bang their heads, their elbows, their knees, she rose up, the silk cloth sliding down her body, her breasts skimming his chest as she pushed herself on top of him. He pulled the silk up and placed his hands on her bottom, and she moved and moved, and all around him the rich dense colours pressed in and filled his head.

When he first started visiting her—that was how he thought of it, "visiting her"—he'd thought they might go for a walk along the seafront, or out into the hills behind the town, or that they might go to one of the little bars that had reopened where he could buy her a coffee or a drink. But that didn't happen. Mostly they didn't leave the cellar. He'd help her clear away the piles of dirt and rock, and then they would retire downstairs. Sometimes they didn't pause, but went to the cellar straightaway. She worked in the middle of what was once the ground floor of the house, on a table he had salvaged for her and on a sewing machine she had somehow obtained, and she slept in the cellar—cooking, eating, and washing at a friend's, someone whose house was more intact than hers. She was back in business, mostly repairs. The women of the town still needed their dresses, the men their shirts and trousers.

He tried to find out more about her. Her English was pretty good—she'd trained as a seamstress in London before the war—and he'd begun to pick up a bit of Italian. He thought girls—women—needed to talk about themselves, needed to be asked questions and gently teased and made to feel pretty, even though Rose was not like that. Girls needed to know your intentions, what you were thinking. He had thought that women wouldn't do the kinds of things that he and Signora Lavelli were doing without having some kind of promise of—he hated to even think it, but still—marriage.

Signora Lavelli wasn't interested in talking. He knew she had suffered great losses in this war. One day, she dumped her handbag onto the bed, looking for her lipstick, and out popped a photograph in a little ornate frame. She was in the photo, seated beside a man, with a small boy on her lap. The child looked exactly like her, the same dark eyes and hair, the same slightly pointy chin—the only difference was whatever it is that makes one face that of a lovely woman and another of a handsome boy. Later Art wished he'd had a better look at the man. She'd reached for the photo and tucked it into the side pocket in her handbag. Then she returned the rest of her belongings to the bag carefully, without looking at Art. He leaned back, propped up on one elbow on the bed, and considered what to say. He wanted to ask what had happened to the boy. He opened his mouth to speak, but she gave him a look of warning, her mouth set in a line. So he ran his hand from her shoulder down to her hand instead. She did not turn away.

Another month passed, and the camp emptied out as every unit that came through left with more personnel than it arrived with. Archie was itching to move out, to head north to the fighting. "I didn't come all this way to sit on my butt," was what he said, what he kept on saying, loud enough to be over-heard by his superiors, making Art wince every time. He'd realized by now that he had no interest in fighting. He'd heard too many grim tales from Langstrom, spent too many nights listening to Milsom's shrieks. His itch to get going, to do something brave, was gone. He was happy to sit on his butt. Especially when he had Signora Lavelli in his lap.

He'd come up with a new routine for his visits—he snuck off after lunch, when the sunshine made everyone a little sleepy. They were supposed to work in pairs, of course, and most of the time they did, one spotting, the other clearing. Two sets of eyes were better than one and you never knew what you might find, from live ordnance to unexploded bombs. Some of the other clearing crews had found body parts in the rubble and the thought of this made Art feel sick; he hoped to hell that never happened to him. Today he was working with Archie in a building that, if you squinted at it from a certain angle, looked undamaged—the facade was almost completely intact. The heavy front door with its gargoyle-head knocker led to a broad hallway wallpapered in black and white, with a delicate wooden side table where someone had left a notebook and an inkwell. But the pen was missing and the ink had spilled, staining the wood. When you walked to the end of the hallway you could see that the rest of the house was gone, blown through to the next street.

They'd eaten their lunch and were lolling in the shade. Sometimes Archie liked to reminisce about being at home, playing with Geronimo, pillaging the neighbour's apricot tree in the summer, playing hockey on the rink in the park in wintertime. Thinking about the town and his family made Art feel so homesick that he wasn't sure what to do with himself. At night alone in his cot he could summon their faces with painful clarity, along with every detail of his house, of his street. But Archie's endless chatter made Art anxious—would he mention his father? Worse, would he mention his father in front of anyone else in camp? Would the unit find out what Art had done?

"I'm going to head off," Art said. "I'll only be gone an hour. Don't do anything 'til I get back."

Archie nodded. "Lucky bastard," he said.

No one could quite believe that Art had managed to find himself a girlfriend in the middle of the war, in Italy, but he had.

"You'll meet a girl one day," Art replied automatically.

"Four kids," Archie said, "that's what I want. One's no good. It's too hard being an only child. Not enough."

"With children, you need scale," Art agreed, as though he knew what he was talking about. "Though, four's too many," he added. He stood up and brushed himself off. "Have a nice snooze," he said as he left Archie leaning against the wall next to his shovel, smoking a cigarette.

Art made his way to Signora Lavelli's a few streets away. When he arrived she was working; he went in for a kiss but she held him at arm's length. She had a job for him; she'd gotten her hands on a big sheet of corrugated iron and wanted him to build a shelter, something that would keep the sun and rain off as she sat at her sewing machine.

Art retrieved the iron sheet from down the hill and eventually managed to get it into place, wedging it into what was left of one of her building's walls and propping up one corner with a column constructed of building fragments, rock and wire. He couldn't stand up to full height in it, and the whole thing leaned at an alarming angle.

"Like Pisa," she said, smiling.

He'd begun to fashion the second column when he heard the explosion. Loud. Signora Lavelli was standing beneath the new makeshift structure and Art dashed over to pull her away;

the column shook but held fast. "Bravo," she said, and she clapped her hands together. But Art was worried. The blast had been nearby. Controlled detonations were not unusual, but as far as he knew nothing had been planned for today. He felt uneasy. He took off toward the explosion.

As he made his way up the hill he met Langstrom. "What was that?" Langstrom asked.

"No idea."

"Where's Archie?"

Art hesitated. "Not sure."

They were supposed to work in pairs.

Art felt a mounting sense of panic.

They rounded another corner and walked into a billowing cloud of dust.

The building he and Archie had been clearing earlier that day no longer existed. The lovely old facade, which had made it through this war and the last, had collapsed. Langstrom ran into the ruins where the great cloud was still rising, climbing over the new layer of rubble, first in one direction, then another. But Art knew where to look; he and Archie had been working in the far corner of the building. Archie was methodical. Dutiful as well. Instead of napping in the shade after lunch, he'd gone back to work, picking up where they'd left off in the morning.

Art climbed over the fallen plasterwork. He spotted a boot. And a few steps further, there was his old friend—lying on top of the wreckage as though he was having that snooze after all. Covered in grey dust like he'd decided to camouflage himself, the way they used to when they were kids playing at war.

Art rushed toward him. If he could pick him up, he could get him to the medic. If he got him to the medic, they could save him. Archie couldn't be dead. It wasn't possible.

Art finished up his war like he'd started it, wielding a shovel and a broom. Guard duty on German POWs was the closest he came to facing down the enemy, his unit always far enough south that the fighting was more rumour than reality. He knew most people would say he was lucky.

Langstrom didn't report Art for having left Archie on his own, and no one blamed Art for what happened. "Even if you'd been there," he'd said to Art that day, "it would have happened anyway. And you'd have been blown up alongside him." Langstrom shipped out less than a week later, and Art felt relieved.

A few weeks after they buried Archie—in the new cemetery at Moro River, alongside the men who'd fought that epic Christmas battle—Lieutenant Milsom went missing. They found his body on the beach a couple of days later.

Signora Lavelli said no to Art's marriage proposal—he knew she would, but he felt that at the very least he should offer to do the right thing. He never did learn her first name. When he saw her for the last time he almost asked, but he couldn't think how to do it without seeming rude, or sentimental, or just plain silly.

The war in Europe ended, and Art prepared to go home to Canada alongside soldiers who had fought in Romagna when heavy rain had turned the Lombardy plain into a muddy swampland; some of them were half-dead, with missing limbs and bandaged heads, or prone, as Lieutenant Milsom had been, to screaming and shivering in the night.

En route, Art wrote his last letter to his family. As usual, he ran out of steam after what seemed to him like a great many words, but on paper was hardly any.

Dear Mum and Dad, Tilly, Peg, Eddie—

I'm shipping out. I'm coming home.
I am wholly unscathed.
Your son and brother,

Private Arthur Lunn

Art assumed the news that he'd been overseas with Archie would have travelled ahead of him. But it hadn't. It seemed that Archie hadn't gotten around to writing to his mother about being stationed with Art, and Art had left that detail out of his own letters, too. When no one said anything about it, not even Peg, Art understood that nobody knew about it, about any of it. And Art wasn't about to tell them.

Art didn't volunteer any information about what he'd done in the war, but people assumed he was a hero anyway. They went ahead and invented their own stories for him. He'd even heard two old biddies whispering behind his back in the ice cream parlour: ". . . had a bad war . . . poor soul . . . terrible things . . ." Those medals that his mother kept in her drawer with her neatly mended stockings and linen sachets of lavender? They were pretty much for good attendance. He'd shown up. He'd spent months in the training camp in Ontario, then was sent to a backwater in Italy where the war had already crushed everything and moved on.

He'd signed up because he'd wanted to do something heroic and now everyone seemed to think he had. He was a fraud. Nobody knew it was his fault Archie died. He'd leave them to their speculation.

After supper his first night back, he helped Tilly wash the dishes, and they swayed side by side to the music on the radio, Tilly humming along.

"I guess you didn't come across Duncan while you were over there?" Tilly asked.

"Who?"

She swatted him with her cloth, leaving a wet patch on his shirt. "My husband! Duncan."

"Oh jeez. I forgot all about him," Art said. "Do you know what he's doing, when he's coming home?"

Tilly shook her head. "No. I haven't heard from him for—well—more than three months."

Art hooked his tea towel around his sister's shoulders and

pulled her into a hug. "He'll be back. You would have heard by now if the news was any different." He had no idea if this was true.

After they finished clearing up, Art went outside to the front steps where Frank and his father were sitting. The warm evening was full of blue smoky light. Art cadged a cigarette off his brother-in-law. A woman Art had never seen before emerged through the front door of the Portman house across the street. "Who's that?" Art asked.

"When she got the news—" his father started to speak then stopped abruptly. "You know about Archie, don't you, son?"

Art nodded, not trusting himself to speak. They really didn't know. He couldn't believe they didn't know.

"When she heard, she decided to sell up and head back east to her family. A sister. Ontario."

The young woman, who was wearing an apron and had her hair tied back with a kerchief, had begun to water Mrs. Portman's roses. She glanced over at them. Art raised his hand.

"Archie Portman isn't coming home," Art's father said, shaking his head as though he still couldn't believe it.

They sat in silence, smoking. What would they think of Art if they learned the truth? He couldn't even begin to think of confessing.

"When do you think Tilly's Duncan might come home, Art?" Frank asked.

This was another thing people did, Art noticed—they asked him questions about the war as though his experience had been anything more than blindly following orders.

"No idea," he replied. "No idea."

Peg came out of the house then, waving the men's cigarette smoke away, coughing dramatically and laughing at herself.

"I saw Rose in town the other day, Art," she said as she sat down next to him.

Rose. "How is she?"

"She's working for her dad now. She said to tell you to head over to Naramata to see her. She said you're welcome any time."

"Oh," said their father, "well there's an invitation."

"All hail the conquering hero," Peg replied. And they all laughed.

Art's entire family was radiating gratitude that he'd been returned to them. He tried to convince himself it was good to be home. If war had taught him anything, it was the importance of moving on, pushing forward, getting up and trying again. He closed his eyes and inhaled. He could smell the lake off in the distance, the fruit ripening in the orchards, Mrs. Portman's flowers across the street. He'd pay Rose a visit.

That summer there was plenty of work. Art got a job labouring for Bob Evans, an orchardist his father knew, up the lake in Summerland. Evans had five acres of apples, rows of carrots and potatoes planted between the trees, and a couple of pigs in a shed behind the house. The land was a stony slope that led down to the foot of the bench, its only advantage the water from a creek that ran to the lake and cut across one corner of the property. Mr. Evans was tender with his trees— he claimed to have dug each and every hole and planted every tree himself. He spent a good part of every morning inspecting the leaves, checking the bark. Art wouldn't have been surprised to learn he'd given every apple a name. Art's job included repairing the old wooden irrigation flumes that funnelled the water from the creek, maintaining the furrows and ditches between the trees, and spraying bug juice using Evans's cranky old hand pump; he spent most of his day soaking wet, hoicking up his workpants which were heavy with mud and chemicals. Though the work was hard, he enjoyed being in the orchard, keeping an eye on the trees; he found himself worrying about whether it was too hot, or too cold, or too dry. At night, he slept on a camp bed in a big canvas tent along with a handful of workers from other farms who Evans rented beds to for a few cents, young men like Art, back from the war with their kit bags and boots, trying to figure out how to be grownups, civilians. Some nights the snoring would wake him up and for a moment he'd think he was still in Italy. And thinking about Italy would lead him to thinking about Archie.

On Sundays Art took the boat across the lake to Naramata to see Rose. She'd come out to meet him with a picnic basket and they'd find a grassy spot by the water, beyond the dock and the fruit-packing house, out of sight. They found it difficult to keep their hands off each other and sometimes they'd have to get into the lake to cool things down. Rose seemed to have changed her mind about Art while he was overseas. He had no idea what had shifted, why she let him court her now when she couldn't—or wouldn't—in the past. And her father, well, it seemed he'd loosened his grip on her as well.

Rose didn't ask about the war, and for that he was grateful. He felt as though when she looked at him she saw good. She saw the part of him that was shining and strong. When he was with her, all that mattered was that moment, the very moment they were living.

One afternoon Art missed the last boat back across the lake. They were lying on a blanket together, holding hands, Art half-asleep, Rose tucked in close at his side. The whistle went and Rose sat up but the boat was already pulling away from the dock.

She gave him a gentle shake. "You missed it," she said.

Art sat up and rubbed his face. He felt heavy in the liquid late-afternoon sunlight. "I guess I'll have to hitch down and spend the night at my folks', get back up to Summerland in the morning."

"Or you could stay here," Rose said. "Get the early boat."

Art's stomach flipped. "Where?" For a moment, he imagined himself in Rose's bed. He didn't think about Signora Lavelli often, but now he remembered how she used to wait for him in the cellar, amidst the bolts of velvet and silk.

"You can sleep in the barn. My folks won't mind."

Art nodded. "Okay. That sounds good."

"And later, when it's dark and everyone's asleep . . ."

Art drew a sharp breath. He looked at Rose. She was smiling broadly.

"Who knows what might happen?" he replied, hoping he sounded smooth, though he felt anything but.

Later that afternoon they made their way along the dusty road, through the orchards and up to Rose's house. The house was not grand but it was large; the front porch alone seemed to contain more furniture—chairs, settees, tables, a comfy-looking swinging bench with its own canopy—than Art's entire house. Rose introduced him to her parents with such formality it was as though they'd never met before. When she said he'd missed the last boat, her father gave Art a grave look, as though this confirmed something he'd always thought about him.

"Oh, what a shame," Rose's mother said. "You're welcome to join us for dinner."

That night, Art took the sleeping roll Rose gave him and bedded down in the hay above where her father kept his horses. The meal had gone all right—Art had kept quiet, only speaking when spoken to, in the hope that Rose's father would think him polite. No one spoke much, in fact—it was as unlike a meal at Art's house as was possible, Rose's mother murmuring to Rose in French when she thought Art might need something—salt, butter, more potatoes. In the hay, Art lay on his back and looked up at the roof of the tidy barn; having a girlfriend meant having to deal with her parents and Art hadn't reckoned with that. He nodded off, wondering what he could do to make Rose's father trust him.

He woke up when he heard the ladder creak; before he could remember where he was, Rose was there beside him.

"I snuck out of the house!" she whispered, triumphant.

"You did!" Art replied, amazed.

It turned out Rose was not shy. Art wondered where he'd got the idea that women were shy: Rose knew what she wanted, just like Signora Lavelli.

The summer continued and Art worked hard for Bob Evans, and slept in Rose's father's barn most Saturday nights. But Art didn't much like the work. He couldn't stand the suspense: Would the damn apples grow? Would the frost arrive too soon? He often found it hard to sleep at night; his dreams were full of explosions and gunshots, blood and dust. He knew soon enough that orcharding wasn't in his blood the way it was in Rose's; she was like a better-looking version of Evans, labouring on the land all day every day. Besides, the season would end before long and he'd have to move on anyway. Finding other work wasn't an issue—there was plenty of work—it was deciding what to do and where to go.

"The railway?" Rose suggested. They were floating on their backs in the lake, holding hands so as to not drift apart. It was a hot afternoon in early September. Art still found it a little strange not to be heading back to school with Eddie, though when his mother had tried to convince him to finish high school he'd ended the conversation quickly. Up and down the valley the hills were brown, the line between the irrigated land and the rest as stark as a desert, the lake oily with runoff, bug spray and heat. The apple harvest was about to commence and Art was bracing himself for it.

"The railway," he replied, shaking his head no. He'd worked so many summers with his father he'd be able to get a job in an instant, but because of that he knew it wasn't for him. When Art was overseas he'd longed to be back home, but it turned out that being in town, surrounded by people who knew him, who knew—or thought they knew—everything about him, made him want to leave again.

"I saw a notice in the paper," he said. "Logging company. Hiring." He'd spotted it in his mother's newspaper the other evening, and he'd gone as far as cutting it out and sticking it in his wallet.

"Logging," said Rose.

"You grow the trees, I'll cut them down."

Rose laughed. Art pulled her through the water toward him. She kissed his neck and then pushed away to swim to the dock.

1956: Toothache

TOOTHACHE. BACK TOOTH, LEFT SIDE, bottom row. The pain felt enormous, like it was a living creature trying to punch its way out through the side of his face. Couldn't keep his tongue from worrying the tooth—and worrying it had brought on a headache behind his eyes, across the bridge of his nose. The steady drip-drip of Scotch from the old canteen his father had given to him a few years back helped a little—the good stuff, just enough during the day to take the edge off without making him foggy on the job. At night, he knocked himself out with the camp hooch the bullcook made with apple cores and potato peelings: jungle brew. This pain had been with him for more than a week now and it wasn't going away.

Art was working as a high rigger, the best-paid job in the woods—a job he'd trained for a while back, if following Scooter Anderson up a tree and ducking as the branches fell down around him counted as training. He'd been working for this particular company for a couple of seasons, first in a railroad logging operation up in Pemberton Valley and now truck logging in from Lillooet Lake, and they were a good outfit. High rigger was reckoned to be one of the more dangerous jobs; Art was promoted from second rigger to high rigger only after Scooter broke his right leg in three places. His safety harness had come undone while he was stripping a backspar, and as he fell he smashed against the tree repeatedly until the guy wires finally stopped his descent, leaving him dangling. Art had to help him climb down the tree using his remaining good leg. Scooter was in such agony he alternated between screaming and passing out. Art braced himself with all he had against the tree, taking his friend's full weight. That was the end of Scooter's logging days.

Art spent most of his time on the job searching out spars. Once he identified a good one, he'd hitch himself to the tree with his rope and hug his way up using his climbing irons— spikes he strapped to his caulk boots. He sliced off branches as he went, transforming the tree into a pole and topping it when he figured he'd got to the right height. Then he'd strip the bark and install the tree plates and steel cables and complicated guy lines—the rigging—at the top, doing his level best not to get tangled up in the lines. Once the spar was rigged, logs could be clipped to the high wire skyline and sent down the mountainside to the landing and the skid road without getting hung up on rocks and windfalls. The road itself was a corduroy of logs laid one next to the other, and the fresh timber was skidded down it, then loaded onto trucks and shifted down to the railway line. The new chainsaws stank of gas and oil but cut so smoothly through the wood it was like the trees were made of ice cream.

Art loved being a high rigger: it was a glamour job, if the forest could be said to have such a thing. He loved being up in the trees, high above everyone and everything. Once he reached the top he'd settle back for a minute or two and survey the view down the mountainside, the river far below. He loved the rough feel of bark, the raw smell of pitch, the dirty glory of the trees themselves, even as he reduced them from multi-limbed strivers reaching for the sun to near-lifeless spars. When he was a kid, he'd loved the idea of monkeys, an animal he'd never seen in real life; now he was the monkey, high up, feeling the flex and strength of his own body.

The thing about logging is that it's noisy: the squealing chainsaws, the loaders, the pickers, the signal horns and the sirens, the trucks with their enormous tires on rough-hewn roads. And the sound a tree makes as it crashes to the ground is like the earth itself cracking open. As though they were logging with dynamite. It had taken Art a while to get used to it; in his early days on the job he'd had to work hard against the urge to flee the noise, but he'd conquered it in the same way he'd conquered his fear of gunfire—by gritting his teeth and pushing through. Nowadays, the noise only really registered with Art when the day was over and the woods fell silent once again—then he'd think, *ah, relief.* But now the pain from his tooth made the cacophony unbearable, as though all the noise, the whole great tumult of it, was being channelled through his mouth. Art needed his wits about him. He was reluctant to take time off, he was reluctant to lose the pay and, even more, he hated giving up his place in the trees for fear that when he returned they'd have hired someone who could work harder, faster. But he was going to have to get out to see a dentist.

Every day in camp was money earned and the money was good, especially for Art with no wife and kids. No house to run, no garden to tend, unlike Peg with her family and her tomatoes, and Eddie out in Calgary, where he'd trained as a mechanic and was now settled down with a young family of his own. The only thing Art owned was his truck. Ordinarily, he could do six weeks in, one week out, much longer than most other guys. This particular job was seasonal—it was early September now and Art reckoned there'd be another six to eight weeks max before snow fell and the operation closed down. He already had a job lined up at Cowichan on the Island in the new year; you could log on the coast all year round, provided you didn't mind working in the unceasing rain. He'd spend a couple of winter months with Rose in Naramata first, if she'd have him. Visit the folks, and Peg, and Tilly's grave.

The camp was located on the north side of the lake and was an unsightly mess: wooden bunkhouses, a cookhouse, a shower block and a blacksmith shop, sheds, the boss's office, the laundry, and broken and redundant machinery, everything piled up on the spot as though there wasn't enough land, when in fact there was nothing but land all around. There were panoramic views of the mountains every which way you looked. The hillside behind had been logged and was littered with branches and stumps and when the wind blew you had to watch out or you might get your head taken off by flying debris. The bunkhouses weren't much better inside: eight men on iron bunks, damp wool Stanfields hanging to dry over the cast iron pot-bellied stove in the corner, a few shelves on the wall to stash their belongings. Some days the smell of socks was almost powerful enough to knock you out. The bullcook and his flunky who were tasked with cleaning were not about to take home any prizes.

Art didn't play cards in the camp; he'd lost his pay packet to the camp card shark a couple of times when he was green, before he'd noticed that most of the older men had wised up and didn't play. This camp didn't have a self-appointed storyteller so when the others were placing bets, Art had taken to reading in the evenings. The cookhouse had a shelf above the hot-water urn that was laden with cheap paperbacks, Westerns and mysteries mostly, the foreman's own collection. Art had been a reader when he was a boy, his mother used to drag them all along to the library above Streatham's Feed Store on Main Street at least once a week. He'd lost the habit when he was overseas, but now found he slipped back into it as though he'd never stopped. He'd lie on his bunk with his hooch and his book, happy.

Civilization was a long way away, accessible only via a

god-awful, rough-cut logging road that led east. Art needed to get on that road in order to see Rose's guy. There was a dentist in Lillooet, but he didn't want to risk it—he'd had a bad experience with a dentist in Merritt last year who had cracked one tooth while pulling out another. Some camps had their own dentist, usually the same fellow who doubled up as the barber, but that didn't even bear thinking about as far as Art was concerned. And he didn't want to end up at the family dentist back home, the French Canadian known as Remy the Remover. That dentist had taken out the teeth of half the adult population of the town, including Art's mother, Peg and Frank. He'd been to visit Peg a couple of weeks after she had hers done. She claimed it was more modern, more hygienic, to have dentures; all real teeth did was crack and decay and cause yet more problems down the line. But Art couldn't endure watching her spit blood into her hankie as the new teeth moved around her mouth, rubbing and chafing. The teeth had altered the way she spoke as well, making her all *caw-caw-caw*, *clack-clack-clack*, pulling her lips back like a horse. He'd had to make an excuse and leave. When he'd complained to Rose, she told him that her mother had scoured the Okanagan to find the best dentist; she'd taken one look at Remy and decided to take her business elsewhere. Art wanted Rose's guy.

It was the end of the work day—if he left now in his truck he could be at the dentist's by morning, even if he pulled off and took a nap somewhere along the way. He'd tell the boss he needed a few days' medical leave and hit the road before it got dark. His record was sterling; he hadn't had to take any days off for—what was it?—five years. Not since Tilly died.

It hadn't occurred to Art that a man might walk out on a marriage. He'd come across loggers who weren't exactly loyal husbands, he'd heard tales about women who weren't model wives, in fact he'd come across one or two of those himself. But to take up with someone else as though the vows you'd made meant nothing whatsoever—it showed how frail the whole institution was, something that perhaps you didn't need to do after all, like go to church, settle down and have a family. His own parents were the exception, of course; they never seemed to disagree about anything—or if they did, they kept it to themselves. Then again, Art's father worked away from home all week; maybe that was the secret of their success. But it hadn't worked that way for Tilly. Turned out her husband, Lieutenant Duncan Wilson, had met a woman when he was stationed in Holland. He brought her back to Canada after the war, and sent Tilly a letter—she hadn't heard from him in over a year and had spent that time in agony, not knowing whether to mourn him—informing her he wanted a divorce. He asked for his grandmother's wedding ring back.

No one in the family had ever met anyone who was divorced. As far as Art knew there were no divorcees in the whole of the Okanagan Valley. Peg told him their parents had lost friends over it. Jimmy Tucker's mother had said it shouldn't be allowed—right in front of Tilly after church one Sunday— and Art's mother had replied, "It's up to you, is it?"

Once the divorce papers were all that remained of the

marriage, Tilly fell ill. She lost her vitality and was possessed by weariness, a tiredness that took her over so completely that getting through the working day became a tremendous trial. By the time Art got home to see her, she'd had to give up her job and her room in the boarding house, and was living with Peg and Frank. The last time he visited, Tilly sat in an armchair with her feet up while Art made tea; her breath was laboured and uneven, her legs and ankles swollen as though her body was full of tears. "Heart condition" was what the doctor had said and Art assumed that meant her heart had been broken. Less than a year later, she died.

His big sister, Tilly, who'd always seemed so much more grown up than the rest of them, who'd been like an extra parent as long as Art could remember: gone. Art wished he had located Duncan Wilson when he was overseas; he should have at least tried to. Or after the war, once Duncan Wilson had asked for the divorce, he should have gone down to Vancouver to find him. Given him a punch or two, knocked some sense into him, dragged him back home to Tilly. But he hadn't done any of that.

Instead, Tilly got divorced, got sick, and died. And there was nothing Art could do about it.

A sharp knock on the window of his truck. Art opened his eyes and closed them again—bright sunlight reflected off the lake up ahead, straight into his face. It was still hot in the Okanagan, no hint of the chill that already gripped the mornings and evenings further north. He was hot, sticky, and sweaty, still in his heavy work clothes, unsure how long he'd been asleep. Rose was standing outside his window, dressed for work in her jeans, her hair pulled up off her face.

"Are you planning on coming inside to say hello," she said as he rolled down the window, "or are you going to stay in there all day?"

He smiled and then winced, raising his hand to his cheek. "Toothache."

She frowned. "You're in the way here, Art." She pointed.

He looked out his rear windshield. A big truck loaded with empty apple crates was right behind him, the driver leaning on his steering wheel with an impatient look on his face. The yard was swarming with workers. Harvest time.

"Shit," said Art. "I'll move."

When he'd arrived late last night Art had been stymied to find Rose's cabin empty, so he'd gone to sleep in the truck. He'd wondered if she'd left the land sometime during the summer and hadn't told him. Art wasn't good at keeping in touch between visits and neither was Rose. But now he could see, straight ahead, under the trees: a brand-new trailer home, silver and white. He drove over and parked his truck beside it.

"You've gone up in the world," he called out to Rose.

"The height of luxury," Rose replied. "Make yourself at home. There's hot running water and everything else a man might need."

Back at the beginning, when the idea that they might behave like a proper courting couple was still a possibility, Rose had suggested they write to each other once a week while he was away working. When Art pointed out that the mail would take about the same amount of time to arrive as he'd be away, given the remote locations of most camps, she said, "Well, I don't care for writing anyway." Rose had this capacity to take a negative and turn it into a victory of sorts; it was one of the things Art admired about her.

He always got home to Rose eventually. If he was lucky, she'd be there, and she'd run at him and jump into his arms, her kiss the sweetest thing. Sometimes when he turned up out of the blue Rose wasn't home; he'd leave her a note and head over to see his folks. Sometimes Rose was home but wasn't so happy to see him—too busy, or simply out of sorts, not willing to put up with him; she'd pour him a cup of coffee and, after he'd drunk it, send him on his way. On those occasions, if he played his cards right, if he smiled at the right moment, he could sometimes talk her round. But if he turned up drunk, as he'd been known to do, relying a little too heavily on the Scotch to get him through the drive, she wouldn't even let him through the door.

Art went up the steps into the new trailer, which was twice the size of Rose's old place. Rose's father had been buying land the past few years from veterans who'd taken up the government's offer of loans for land and then changed their minds about farming once they'd spent a year or two at it. Rose and her father figured the only way to make the business of orcharding viable was to have scale. Clearly their tactic was beginning to pay off. The trailer had a new-car smell to it, but apart from that, it did not resemble any trailer home Art'd ever been in. There was a seating area with a wide built-in chesterfield and a coffee table, a full wall of shelves for Rose's books and records. The bedroom had an actual bed in it and the compact bathroom had a shower and a sink.

Art stripped off his layers, his flannel shirt, his boots, his paraffin-coated workpants so stiff with sweat and dirt they could stand up by themselves. It was cool and dim in the trailer, which was positioned under a canopy of old umbrella pines closer to the lake than her old cabin. She stepped in through the door as Art was pulling off his socks.

"Make yourself at home," she said again, laughing.

"Come here, you," Art replied, grabbing her hand and pulling her into an embrace. He pushed himself up against her snugly and she moulded her body to his.

She slipped her hand under the waistband of his shorts. "I have to go straight back out," she said. She pushed her hand down further.

He took a deep breath, his face in her hair, which was pulled back into a neat ponytail.

She stepped away from him. "Gotta go."

Art moaned. "Come here."

She shook her head. "The dentist's name is McCoy—he's in Kelowna. There's a pay phone over at the gas station."

"Naramata joins the twentieth century," Art said, but Rose had already stepped back out to her apples and her crew.

That night Art was kept awake by his aching tooth—the rye and seven he'd drunk with Rose hadn't helped him sleep. In the morning he left early, drove his truck up the highway and took the car ferry across the lake to Kelowna. The problem with the Okanagan was it was too damn sunny—Art was in a fog of booze and pain and the sunshine compounded it. He hadn't been able to eat much for a week now; last night Rose had fed him soup with his drink. The trailer was comfortable and she'd made the sleeping area nice with gauzy curtains and pillows and candles, which Art appreciated after the sparse comforts of camp. In the golden light, he'd stroked her back as she stretched out on the bed beside him.

The storefront sign read "McCoy's Modern Dentistry." There was a good-looking blonde in reception and the place didn't smell of blood and sawdust, which Art found reassuring. In fact, the interior of the dentist's office was modern, gleaming chrome and shining white porcelain sinks and a fancy black-leather reclining chair for patients. There were no sets of dentures on display. McCoy examined Art's mouth—"I'm examining your mouth now"—gave him a shot of lidocaine—"I'm giving you a shot of lidocaine now"—and fixed the tooth temporarily—"This is temporary. You'll have to come back to see me again." There was no screaming and only a tiny amount of blood. Art left with a prescription and a follow-up appointment for two months' time.

Art wandered down the street—it was still early and most of the stores weren't open yet—and into a coffee shop where he sat at the counter and drank a Coke through a straw without first needing to steel himself. His mouth felt numb and rubbery and weird, but even that was a huge improvement. His head was clearer already, and even his shoulder and neck muscles, which had ached with the tension of staving off the pain, were beginning to relax.

As he walked up to the till to pay, the door of the coffee shop opened. A tall, thin man entered. He took off his smart black hat and jacket and hung them on the stand, straightened his tie, and walked past Art—passing just inches away—to take a seat at the counter.

Art felt the hair on the back of his neck stand up.

"Mister?" The girl behind the till was waiting for Art to pay. He handed her a quarter. Then he turned back to look at the man.

It was him.

It was Mister Theodore.

He looked the same. Older, a little more filled out. Better colour—his skin no longer yellow. Better dressed. Prosperous.

"Here's your change, mister," the girl said.

Art looked at her.

She held the money in her outstretched hand.

He took the coins and slipped them into his pocket.

As Art opened the door to leave, he turned to the man one more time. It was really him.

He stepped across the threshold and let the coffee shop door shut behind him.

Art couldn't make himself walk down the street. But he couldn't turn around and go back into the coffee shop either—if he did, what would he do? What would he say? He put his hat on. His jaw felt loose, his face misaligned. He opened his mouth—his skin felt stretched tight over the bones of his face. He hadn't thought about the past for a long time.

There was a bench in front of the coffee shop, in the shade. Art sat down and tried to think. Mister Theodore wouldn't know him from Adam—the last time they'd met Art had been a little boy. He could go in there and deck him and walk back out again—and Mister Theodore would be none the wiser. Or he could go in there and remind the man of the whole sorry saga and what it had cost him, what it had cost the town, and Mrs. Portman and Archie—and then deck him. His head began to pound, he could feel his pulse beating in his temples, and he realized with horror that what he was feeling was fear, as though if he went back in there to confront Mister Theodore there was a chance the man would grab him and hog-tie him and humiliate him all over again. He patted his pockets, looking for his canteen, then realized he'd forgotten it at Rose's.

And then the door of the coffee shop opened, and Mister Theodore came out. He walked over to a car—a shiny red Buick—and placed his jacket and hat on the back seat before climbing into the driver's seat. He started the engine, pulled out, and drove away.

Another ten minutes passed before Art felt steady enough to stand up and make his way to his truck.

He parked in front of the house his father had built. He sat for a moment, amazed once again at how small it was. How had four kids fit in there all those years?

Woodruff Avenue was empty. Art felt a kind of heaviness, not brought on by the dentist's lidocaine but by the pressure of the past. He always felt this when he came home, as though a storm was brewing out over the lake. Being with his family made Art restless. This was the condition of his life, he knew it now, always wanting to leave as soon as he'd arrived. But knowing it was part of him, recognizing it, didn't make it any easier.

He climbed out of the truck at the same time his mother emerged from the front door of the house. She was wearing her apron, which he could see was dusted with flour. Art felt like he was seven years old again.

"I made cheese scones to have with the soup," she said. Her tone had sharpened after Tilly died and now she often sounded angry even when she wasn't.

"Did you know I was coming?"

"No." She rested her hand on his arm gently.

"You've got those work boots on," she said, making him follow her round the side of the house to the back door, past the big old lilac with its few remaining, now brown, blooms.

"I'm clean!" he protested but of course he obeyed and took

his boots off on the back porch. Inside, the house smelled the same—coal, fresh bread, furniture polish. He placed his boots on the mat by the door and noticed the absence of his father's boots—he hadn't retired yet but was planning on doing so later that year. Art answered his mother's questions—she approved of the fact that he was a member of the union and in near-constant work—as she stood by the stove stirring the simmering soup. He drank tea that she served him in one of her fancy cups, as though he was a special guest, and he felt stupidly pleased by this gesture. He used the little silver spoon to give the tea a dainty stir.

There was a noise on the back porch. Through the screen door Art could see Peg and her friend Nancy loaded down with wooden apple crates. Nancy and Peg, same as ever. Many of the kids they grew up with had moved across the province, the country, for work; even Eddie had gone. Their sleepy orchard town hadn't grown after the war, hadn't thrived in the way it might have done. It was the kind of place young people left behind.

"Art!" Peg shouted. "Open the door!"

"Say 'please,'" said their mother.

"Please! Before I drop this crate."

Once he'd taken the crates from the women and stacked them on the floor, he gave his sister a hug. It was one of the good things about coming home—giving Peg a hug. She looked good. She'd gained a little weight. Gave a bit more heft to her bustling. Three kids, so she was always bustling.

Nancy, of course, looked even better. Art wasn't sure exactly when Nancy had become a looker. Around about the time she married that Italian who'd arrived in town with an espresso coffee machine that he fussed over and boasted about as though he'd invented the damn thing. It felt strange to Art that Nancy had married an Italian. It made him worry a little that—what was his name? Luigi, but everyone called him Louie—would somehow know where Art had been stationed during the war, would put the dates together with the place and figure out that Art couldn't possibly have seen battle, couldn't be a war hero. But Louie turned out to be a northerner who was as determined as Art not to talk about the war. And he'd transformed that coffee machine into a successful European foods import business, distributing goods up and down the valley.

"Nancy," Art said, nodding his head in her direction, the air between them a little thicker than it should be.

Nancy blushed. "Art."

"To what do we owe this visit?" Peg asked.

He pointed at his mouth. "Dentist."

"Should have taken my advice," she said, and she clacked her dentures at him.

"Thank you for picking up the apples for me, girls," said Art's mother as she pulled some coins out of her apron pocket.

"I don't need your money," said Nancy.

"I set it aside. Take it," his mother said.

Nancy rolled her eyes at Art and put her hand out.

"Peg," his mother said next.

Peg also accepted the money dutifully.

Always pay your debts. His mother didn't say it, but she might as well have. "Now say 'thank you,'" she said.

Peg and Nancy both gave little curtsies.

"You're just in time for lunch," his mother added.

"I'm off, Mrs. Lunn—I need to get back to the house. I left Louie with the youngest."

"Well, that's a shame," Art's mother said.

Art held the back door open for Nancy and as she left she brushed past him a little more closely than was necessary.

While they ate—Art stuck to the soup, his mouth not quite ready for the rigours of a scone—Peg passed on her news, the progress of the children as well as Frank's promotion to principal. Frank, her white-collar husband. Art looked at his sister and wondered how she had become this woman, capable and well-organized, neat in her practical skirt, expert at sewing and pickling and jam-making, with her committees and her meetings. His mother was the same and Tilly had been once too—robust and cheery engines of domestic activity. But there were other ways for women to be. He thought of Rose with her sharp business brain and her ambitions for her land and her orchards.

As though she'd read his mind, Peg asked, "How's Rose?" The two women weren't friends, but their paths crossed from time to time. As far as Art could tell Rose didn't really have friends, not like Peg whose life was crowded with them.

"She's fine. She's doing well."

"Bumper crop of apples this year."

"So they say."

"Speaking of which," Art's mother said, "would you go fetch the apple boxes from the cellar for me, Art? I'll get this fruit wrapped and stored this afternoon so Peg can return the crates."

Art got up from the small kitchen table, a crook in his back; he'd been sitting hunched up on one of his mother's too-small kitchen chairs. Everything was too small in this house. The freezing in his mouth had almost worn off and his jaw ached mildly. He was glad to be given a task, a reason to do something useful. Once he'd done something useful, he could leave.

Art still hated the cellar, even with its new electric light. When he was a kid he did his best to avoid it, despite the allure of the child-sized door and its potential as a place to hide. When other kids talked about digging a hole to China— why did kids think that was a good idea?—Art would think about the root cellar and how it must be halfway to China already. But he never suggested digging there.

Art latched the cellar door open, using the hook his dad had installed so the door wouldn't blow shut while he was inside, trapping him in the dark. He was hoping he could simply reach in with one arm and drag out the apple boxes, but when he switched on the light he could see they were neatly stacked at the back of the space.

He bent down low and made his way in, immediately banging his head on the same beam he'd banged his head on countless times. It was best to crawl, but Art couldn't bear it, the feel of the gritty floor beneath his hands and knees, so he stayed on his feet, bent forward ninety degrees. He grabbed the boxes, their waxy cardboard making them difficult to grip, and as he turned back to the door, he hit his head on the lightbulb that hung from the ceiling on a cord, making it swing round and round, casting wild shadows, until Art caught it, burning his hand in the process. He sat down in the dirt, defeated.

Mister Theodore. The man from the jungle. It was more than twenty years ago. But down here in this dark cramped space, it felt much more recent. He thought of the strawberry jam he'd taken from the shelf behind his head years ago. Why hadn't he approached Mister Theodore this morning? Taken the opportunity to tell him off, to set the record straight, to . . . to what?

He'd missed his chance to confront the man. He'd missed his chance to exact revenge, however minor.

After lunch Art insisted on giving Peg a ride home, despite the fact that she lived four blocks away and said she wanted to walk. Once in the truck, instead of turning left he turned right, and headed in the direction of the bench above the lake.

"Let's go visit Tilly," he said.

Peg gave him a look, but she didn't object. She rolled down the window and took a deep breath.

"The kids are still swimming," she said.

"I remember that," Art replied. "Being back at school and knowing that winter is coming but it's still warm enough to swim in the lake. I loved that. It felt—I don't know—illegal or something."

"Sometimes I go for a swim during the day. I don't tell Frank."

"Why not?"

"I don't know. It's too glorious. I feel guilty. Him in the office, me in the water."

"Peg and her love affair with the lake."

"Housewife Neglects Duties to Throw Herself in the Drink."

Art laughed.

"I try not to be seen, but it's hard. Town this size."

"Everybody knows, Peg. Everybody."

The graveyard sloped gently to the low bluff, at the bottom of which lay the railway tracks. Beyond was the glinting lake—and all around them, to the north and to the south, the summer-dry brown hills of the Okanagan Valley. Art drove around the loop, past the older section with its crumbling gravestones, where the road was lined with big oaks and drooping willows, to the modern section where their sister was buried. Tilly's stone was laid flat in the well-groomed grass. Art and Peg got out of the car.

It was wrong that Tilly was dead: worse than that, it was unnatural. It was all so damn heavy, the weight of remembering, the weight of living.

"When Tilly lived with us, before she died, Frank and I used to sit with her in the evenings. I'd darn socks, she'd knit, and Frank would smoke. She liked to talk about Duncan

Wilson, how those few weeks they spent together in Vancouver were the best weeks of her life."

"I'd like to throttle that guy," Art replied.

"Wouldn't bring her back," Peg replied.

"I used to look forward to Tuesdays so much," he said.

"Tuesdays?"

"The day that Rose would meet me at Tilly's."

Peg smiled.

"Even now, I love Tuesdays."

"When are you gonna marry her, Art?"

Art didn't reply. He'd thought about it, of course he had. But, well, the timing hadn't been right. And now, after all this time, he wasn't sure Rose would want to marry him. He couldn't give her the life she wanted, whatever that might be. And he couldn't face asking her and being turned down— that would be too humiliating. He saw a shadow of himself in Duncan Wilson. Maybe the best way to honour his commitments was not to make any. And things with Rose were fine as they were.

Art and Peg stood for a while, looking out over the lake. There was a steamboat in the distance. He remembered the first summer he worked with his dad. The crew had been working ten miles or so out of town and at the end of every day, Art was allowed to ride the handcart by himself all the way to the station. He pumped the handcart as fast and hard as he could, listening out for distant signal explosions in case a train was coming down the line. Whenever he passed the top of the ravine on the Templeton land he'd look down into it and imagine he could see the men, in their lean-tos, around their campfires. But of course by that point they were long gone.

He thought now about telling Peg about Mister Theodore. She'd be amazed to hear he'd seen him; she'd want to know every last detail. But she would also wonder why Art hadn't confronted him. They had never talked about what happened in the jungle, not since the night Mr. Portman died. Their whole family had stuffed it away as though it had never happened. What good would come from rehashing it all now? They'd never talked about it, and probably never would.

Art arrived back in the camp early the following morning. He'd driven in past the boss's hut where a light shone, but the bunkhouses were all dark. He turned off the truck's engine and sat for a few minutes listening to it cool down. He had his truck windows open and the night air poured down off the mountains, bringing with it the sharp smell of tree resin, of the forest they were felling. Art chomped his teeth together a few times, relieved the pain was nearly gone. He'd stocked up on bourbon and Scotch in town before driving out to say good-bye to Rose; at least now he could get back to drinking for the sake of drinking instead of wasting it on pain control.

One by one, lights came on in the bunkhouses. Art continued to sit in his truck, listening to the camp wake up. Peace. If he belonged anywhere, it was here, off a road from nowhere that led to nothing but trees.

—

There were three crews operating at three different cut sites, and they were busy hauling out the logs and transporting them to the railway where they'd begin their epic journey through the mountains to Howe Sound, down at Squamish.

Art's crew had moved to a new cut site while he was away, more than an hour's drive from camp. The men headed out straight after breakfast and for once Art was grateful for the non-stop banter—he didn't need to talk, but he didn't need to think, either.

The new block was yet another steep slope dense with trees. As Art climbed he assessed what he saw—the first set of high-wires had been installed by another rigger while he was away but nothing had been cut yet. There was a great deal of old growth here, nothing compared to the size of the trees on the coast, but enough huge pine and fir and spruce to make this tough terrain worth logging. Art got on with it.

Four weeks later, Art woke to the first proper snowfall of the year, white flakes illuminating the dark morning. The place was transformed—the truck that had been stripped of its parts and was resting on its axis, the jerry-built lean-tos, the rows of bunkhouses, the splintered tree stumps, the garbage from the cookhouse, the mud and the dirt were all shrouded by a thick layer of white. Over the next couple of weeks the camp would reduce to a skeleton crew; they'd move the machinery into storage and then close down for the winter. The forest would fall silent once again.

—

Rose figured out she was pregnant one Sunday in February as Art was getting ready to head to the coast for a new job.

He'd been with her all winter. It was the longest they'd spent together and they'd fallen into a comfortable routine. He'd been surprised to find how easy it was to adjust to life away from the company of men, even after a decade of logging. He wasn't completely undomesticated, his mother had made sure of that—he could rustle up bacon and eggs, and a grilled cheese sandwich. Food of the gods. And there was plenty of work to do. He overhauled the generator when it stopped working and built an outside furnace when he realized the little wood-burning stove in the trailer didn't generate much heat. When he first arrived, before the ground froze, he built an outhouse as well, to give them both a bit more privacy. Rose spent most days in her father's basement office; they were negotiating another land deal. In the evenings they'd listen to music, Art with his head in Rose's lap, and they'd talk through their plans for the next day, the following week.

That Sunday in February began like any other. Rose went to her parents' for dinner, same as always, and Art stayed home, put a Miles Davis record on—Rose was trying to convince him jazz was a good thing—and read through a few back issues of *Life* magazine. He'd thought about driving over to visit his folks but had decided against it. His parents knew where he was staying, everyone knew where he was staying, but nobody said a word, as though as long as the situation wasn't discussed it wasn't really happening. Art suspected Rose's parents weren't quite so willing to turn a blind eye. He had this notion that Rose's father was a bit of a bully, that he tried to keep a tight rein on both Rose and her mother even as he allowed his daughter to work and live alone. In the years since Rose had moved out, to the old cabin and now to this trailer, he'd seen even less of her parents than when they were kids. Rose's mother's illness, whatever it was, seemed to have become even more debilitating of late. Art hadn't had many opportunities to convince them of his charms, though truth be told he didn't think they were open to convincing.

Sometimes when Rose came back from her parents' she'd be very quiet and it would take her a bit of time to settle in once again. When she got home that night she sat in the car for a while. Art heard her pull up and came out to wait for her at the top of the steps. It was a clear, cold night, the moon and stars reflecting off the lake. When she finally got out of the car, it was clear she'd been crying. She brushed past him on her way inside, and sat down without taking off her coat.

He sat beside her and took her hand.

"I'm going to have a baby," she said.

Art drew a breath. A baby. He realized he'd known already— something in the way she smelled, tasted, moved. He had a job lined up on the Island; he was due to head out in a couple of days. He didn't know what to say.

"We don't have to get married," Rose said. She gripped his hand.

He couldn't help but laugh at how emphatically she said it, as though she was saying they didn't have to die.

"We don't?"

"Why should I have to get married? I'm my own woman," she said.

"Most people want to get married," Art said, mildly, "especially when . . ."

"I'm not a kid who's got herself into trouble, Art. I don't need to be rescued. Besides, I knew this could happen."

"You knew this could happen?"

"Art, what we do," she gave him a nudge, "well, that's how grown-ups make babies."

He laughed. Art had thought he didn't want to get married either. And he understood that Rose was not in need of rescuing. However, he knew full well that he'd be hard-pressed to find anyone in town who'd agree with that. Least of all her parents. He wanted to do right by Rose. He didn't want to see her—and the baby—shunned, for their lives to be made difficult. He didn't want to be Duncan Wilson.

"Come on, Rose," he said, "won't you marry me?"

And he believed it then: It was right. They could be happy.

"You don't have to marry me," she replied.

"That's not what I'm saying—I'm asking, will you marry me?"

Rose sighed. She turned toward him and gave him a kiss.

"You're the only man I've ever known," she said, "who didn't assume I'd be desperate to get married. I don't want to get married. I'm my own woman," she repeated.

Does she not want to get married, he thought, *or does she not want to marry me?*

—

Out on the coast, Art couldn't settle into the work. The camp was the biggest he'd ever seen; it had grown considerably since he'd last worked on the Island four or five winters ago. Back then it had consisted of a few buildings on a log-float. Now the camp was laid out along the shoreline like a frontier town in its own right, row after row of bunkhouses with separate two-storey accommodations for the Chinese and Hindu mill workers. A brand-new kraft pulp and paper mill had been constructed a few miles up the coast; and here the sawmill sprawled across a couple of acres with its own port and railway. The sawdust burners, like giant, rusty upside-down badminton birdies, glowed red night and day, belching out smoke, and the diesel and gas engines supplying power ran until late in the evening. The mountains that hemmed the camp trapped in smoke and oily fumes and a dreadful rotting smell from the pulp mill. To Art, accustomed to the sparse functionality of backwoods camps in the interior, it was a version of hell.

Art's crew was working inland, patch logging on the side of a mountain about ten miles north, and every morning he was glad to leave the camp behind. The trees on the island were enormous and grew so quickly you could practically hear them. Rigging took him up higher than ever before but the views were disappointing—most of the time the slopes were socked in with low clouds and mist. He found the incessant rain depressing. It seeped into his boots and down the back of his neck, despite his waterproofs. The bunkhouse drum heater didn't pump out enough heat to dry the clothes the men strung across the rafters, so everything was always damp, and nothing smelled good. For the first time since the war, Art felt homesick. But this time, the thing he missed was Rose. He hated being away from her. He wondered how she was feeling. He was sure she wouldn't be having an easy time of it, not with her father, not with the town and the way people there could be. He thought of Tilly, and how ashamed she'd been by the divorce. And he thought about Archie, growing up without his father, no man around the house.

After three months, Art handed in his notice. On the way home he drove into downtown Vancouver, to Birks on the corner of Granville and Georgia, where he bought Rose a diamond ring.

Later that summer, Art and Rose got married at the registry office in Vancouver without telling anyone back home. They'd left just after midnight in order to arrive in the city by morning, the night warm and silent. Rose fell asleep in the truck almost immediately and Art couldn't stop himself from glancing over at her. Rose. Marrying him. Carrying his child.

He'd proposed it to her as more of a strategic alliance than a marriage.

"An alliance?" Rose had said.

"Well, you could keep doing what you're doing, building up this business. And I could keep doing what I'm doing," he waved a hand in the air as though to encompass the logging and the drinking and the other women he thought she must know about. "But we'd make it formal. That way you won't catch any flack. Your folks will be happy. My folks will be happy. The kid will have two lawfully wedded parents. You'll still be your own woman. And I'll be my own man."

"You make it sound so appealing."

"I don't mean that we wouldn't still be . . . us. We'd be the same two people we've always been. Think about it. It could make things easier for us both."

"You don't want to give up logging."

"No." Give up logging? Where had that come from? "No," he shook his head. "But I'd come home more often. I'd take shorter contracts closer to home, longer breaks."

Rose nodded slowly. "It's true, it would make things easier. I'd no longer wonder what people are saying behind my back as I walk down the street. I wouldn't have to hide from your sister when I see her in town. We could keep our business separate and I could take care of your finances and, well," she cleared her throat, "there are advantages. I can see that."

"Keep our business separate?"

"You're bad with money, Art."

It was true. He made good money but he spent it quickly. And he knew Rose was serious about her orcharding business. "Reinvest" was practically her favourite word, and she was working toward buying her father out one day. Whereas Art didn't care about money, as long as he had enough to splash around when he drove out of the forest and into town.

"You hide when you see Peg?"

"She's so nice to me, I can tell she feels sorry for me."

"For what?"

"For the fact that her brother has tarnished my reputation."

"I didn't know you have a reputation, Rose," he said.

"Well, Art, thanks to you, it seems I do." She paused, then said, "It's not like I want a big house and a station wagon, and for us both to start going to church on Sunday."

Art kissed her neck. "You do want those things, though, really. Women want those things."

"It's you who wants all that," she said, laughing.

They'd decided to get married in Vancouver—neither of them had wanted their families to fuss. Once they'd made up their minds to do it, they both just wanted to get it done. Art had corralled a fellow logger, Bob Nestor, into acting as a witness at the wedding. He'd known Nestor for a long time; they'd worked together on and off since Art's first job logging—it had been Nestor's first contract as well. Like Art, he'd been overseas and arrived home unsure of what to do with himself. He'd left logging a few years back and was working in Vancouver—Art wasn't entirely sure doing what. He wouldn't describe Nestor as a friend exactly; there was something about him he didn't quite trust, though he couldn't put his finger on what. But Nestor had three things going for him: he wasn't from home so he wouldn't blab about the wedding, he lived in Vancouver, and Art knew his phone number.

They had arranged to meet outside the registry office. Nestor brought along his girlfriend, a young Native woman named Lorette. Nestor and Lorette looked terrific, like they were the ones getting married, Nestor in a dark suit, white shirt and tie, Lorette in a yellow dress with a big wide skirt. In contrast, Art's single pair of dress pants were a little too small for him, tight around the waist, and Rose was eight months pregnant with only one dress that fit, navy blue with a little white collar that she said made her look like a fancy pork chop with a paper frill. Art had bought both Rose and Lorette white rose corsages straight from the florist's chill cabinet, and in the heat of the August day they gave off a frosted mist that made Rose's cheeks glow even pinker than they already were.

The ceremony was comically brief, conducted by a man who looked like an undertaker, followed by the signing of the marriage certificate, and that was that, they were husband and wife. They took themselves off to the Hotel Georgia where Art had booked a room for the night; in the bar Nestor ordered champagne, which none of them had ever tasted before. They downed it like it was fizzy lemonade before moving on to highballs.

"Well, you've done it now," Nestor said to Art.

Art nodded solemnly. He had. They had. He took Rose's hand. Like him, she was wearing a wedding band now, along with her engagement ring.

"It's downhill all the way from here," Nestor added. He turned to Rose, "No offense, Mrs. Lunn."

"Nonsense," said Art. "Uphill. We're going uphill, aren't we, Rose?"

She laughed. "I don't know which sounds worse. I can barely drag myself off the couch these days."

"You're going to be so happy," said Lorette. "It's so romantic."

Art looked at her. She couldn't be much more than twenty.

"And," she added, "a baby! I've always wanted a baby."

Nestor guffawed and put his hands up. "Don't look at me, lady."

Art turned to Rose. She winced; maybe the baby had kicked her again. He found it alarming, how she was growing bigger, the size of whatever it was she was incubating. He couldn't begin to imagine how she would deliver such a thing. But at least he'd managed to get her to marry him. If he'd only ever done the right thing once in his life, this was it.

That night in the enormous hotel bed, surrounded by dense clouds of pillows, Art couldn't sleep. Too wound up from the momentous events of the day, and on edge from Rose's thunderous pregnant snoring, he found himself thinking about Archie. Private Archie Portman, in his Italian grave. "What does she see in you?" Archie used to ask, back when they were still in high school. "I'm serious, what on earth does Rose see in you?"

"You think she's too good for me?" Art asked.

"Yes," Archie snorted. "Much too good for you!"

And Art had to agree. Even now, still, Art had to agree.

She arrived in early September, when summer still lingered on the lake. They decided to name her Celeste, which Art thought was the most sophisticated-sounding name he had ever heard; he found himself repeating it over and over again, as though the name itself was possessed of a kind of star-filled magic. She had blue eyes and a shock of black hair that stood on end despite Rose's soft attempts to smooth it. They took her home from the hospital in the truck and Art carried her gingerly up the steps behind Rose who was sore and tired. He gave Celeste a tour of the trailer and the orchard, and after that he took her down to the lake. She was calm and still and warm in her blanket and Art thought she seemed impressed by her surroundings. "There's the lake," he said, "I'll teach you to swim. I'll teach you to row a boat and catch a fish and chop down a tree. The important things in life."

They were subject to a relentless flood of well-wishers, spearheaded by his mother and Peg, bearing gifts of tiny clothes and hats and booties. Rose's mother rallied and arrived to help out every morning as Art was getting ready to drive to work. He'd been working a summer contract logging a large block east of Oliver, which meant he could live at home.

At night Rose took Celeste from her tiny cot into their bed to nurse her. Art liked to wake up with Rose so he could lie there listening to the sound of Celeste snuffling, Rose breathing. He learned how to change a diaper; this turned out to be a straightforward task, provided you timed it right and had all the necessary tools available. He'd never much enjoyed spending time with babies, even Peg's and Eddie's; the trouble was that they were wobbly and insubstantial and if you held them wrong it felt as though their heads might fall off. But Celeste was different. Of course she was.

The summer contract ended and Art took a job further north, logging on the south side of Big White Mountain where a ski hill had opened up a few years before. The snow came early that year and Rose grew nervous about Art driving home in the dark, even though the new floating bridge at Kelowna cut the journey time considerably. The drive was often hairy. One night the snow came down so hard Art couldn't see the road ahead; he had to keep getting out of the truck to make sure he wasn't about to head off the side of a cliff. The trip took five hours instead of two. When he opened the door of the trailer, Rose was at the table, Celeste asleep in her arms. Art took off his boots and sat down on the couch; he was weary. Rose brought the baby over to him and he leaned back and closed his eyes.

"You need to stay in camp," she said. "Just during the week. Just while there's snow."

"I know," he said. "I know."

Most of the guys he'd started logging with after the war had since moved on to other jobs: they'd gone back to school, or they'd found work that was less brutal, that let them live at home with their wives. But Art wasn't ready to do that. He didn't know if he'd ever be ready.

So, he moved up to the camp. It was a small outfit, truck logging, clearing a block of easy terrain, scrappy pines and firs, crown land a couple of miles in from the highway. A lot of the loggers lived in Kelowna, forty miles west. There were six half-empty bunkhouses and Art had only one roommate, a kid named Todd who was fresh out of high school. Todd had never worked away from home before and cried himself to sleep most nights. Art tried to be fatherly toward him, but his heart wasn't in it. If he had to listen to someone cry, it should be Celeste.

Weekends were precious. Most Fridays he got home in time for supper, unless the road conditions were bad. Celeste was usually asleep in her cot by the time he got in and he'd lie on the bed next to her for a while, breathing the air she breathed, listening to her baby noises, leaving the camp and the work and the road behind. Rose always put on her favourite dress, and her perfume, and a bit of lipstick, and when he got up he'd have a shower and a shave. Then he'd help Rose cook dinner, Art chopping while Rose stirred. They'd put on a record with the volume turned low and sit together, and Art felt they were each as surprised as the other to have found themselves a family.

Art arrived back in camp at the end of a working day marked by the first rainfall of the season—all surfaces were immediately covered in a thick coat of mud, as though it had been raining for weeks. His workpants were heavy with it. He decided he'd peel off his layers, have a shower and head over to the cookhouse. But before he even managed to take off his boots, Todd rushed in.

"You gotta go to the foreman's office," he said, bursting with urgency. "You gotta head over there straightaway."

Art ran across camp and up the rickety steps into the foreman's portacabin. The foreman was behind his desk, his face grim.

"You need to phone home," he said.

"Home?" Art said. Rose didn't have a phone, though rumour had it that phone lines were going to be put in along the road in the summer. The camp didn't have a phone either; messages came in via radio.

The foreman handed Art a piece of paper. "Your wife. Head office relayed it—you need to head into town and call that number." Art looked at it: Rose's parents'.

The nearest phone was at a gas station on the outskirts of Kelowna, but before Art reached it he decided to drive all the way home instead of calling. The rain had washed away most of the snow from the highway and he made good time, the heating turned up high in the hope that his clothes might dry out a little. When he pulled up outside the trailer, he could see that it was dark, no lights to indicate they were home. He went inside anyway, hoping to find them there, tucked up together, sleeping. The place was empty and in a state of disarray, dishes on the counter, the bed unmade, as though Rose had left in a hurry.

He drove up to Rose's parents' place. These days they lived on ranchland spread out across the hills; Rose's father's attention had shifted from orchards to horses. Since Celeste came along Art had been over there more often. Her parents had more time for him now that he'd married their daughter and produced a child, though he was pretty sure Rose's father would never actually trust him. The road up to their house was pitted, the potholes full of rainwater; Art had offered to help Rose's father re-grade the drive in the spring.

It was raining harder than ever and when he got out of the truck an enormous wave of thunder rolled down into the lake below. The light was on above the front door and Art knocked. He took a deep breath in an effort to calm down, to prepare himself for whatever was happening. Rose's mother opened the door, and when he saw her, Art realized he'd assumed she had died. But here she was—alive but looking dreadful, her normally immaculate posture abandoned, her hair unbrushed. She didn't greet Art, but shuffled to one side so he could enter the house. When he walked into the front room, he saw Rose's father in his armchair and Rose herself on the chesterfield under a blanket, lying there staring at the ceiling, not moving, as though she'd been kicked in the ribs by one of her father's horses and was in too much pain to get up. He pulled up a chair and sat down beside her.

"Rose," he said, "what is it?" But he already knew.

"Celeste," she said, her voice full of emotion. "Celeste . . ." She turned her face away from Art, as though she couldn't bear to look at him.

Rose's mother delivered the news, her voice low, her accent thicker than usual, almost indecipherable. But Art understood what she said. Celeste had died in her cot. When Rose woke up after an unaccountably long and deep sleep, she reached over to pick up their baby. Celeste was cold and still. The doctor said this sometimes happened: there was no reason.

"God gives," Rose's mother said, "God takes away."

But Art could think of a reason. He was not a religious man, but he knew this was a reckoning. It had been waiting, biding its time, all these years. Celeste had been given to him and now she had been taken away. Why had he believed he could be happy? His baby. His Celeste. The person who had shown him he could provide and be provided for, he could love and be loved.

In that moment, Art was pulled under the dock by the lake monster. He was gunned down by a man without hope beside a railway car. He was blown up by a stray bomb in Italy. He was strangled by his own guy wires as he slipped from his perch on the highest tree in the forest. Except this was worse, much worse. He was alive and their baby was gone.

There was no way out, no return to life before Celeste, not for him, and not for Rose. He sat down, mud beginning to flake off his workpants, and he realized he had no idea what to say or what to do. There was no way back to light and air and living.

1968: Birthday

ART CLEANED HIMSELF UP in the motel outside Chilliwack. In the bathroom mirror, which was flecked with toothpaste from a previous occupant, he thought he looked pretty good. Not bad for nearly forty-one. He didn't have to suck in his gut because he didn't have a gut in the first place. He was tired and his head ached, but that was nothing a swig of Listerine and a couple of aspirin couldn't cure. Or, indeed, a stiff drink. He was wearing a new pair of black slacks and a blue shirt he'd managed to buy in a menswear store in Nanaimo last week in between epic stints with Sal. Gail? Sal. He had intended to drive all the way to the Okanagan in one day—straightforward enough if you get an early ferry off the island—but he'd left it too late and was halfway up the Fraser Valley yesterday afternoon before realizing he was still drunk. So he'd pulled over and into this motel.

Well, he was sober now. And today: today was his mother's birthday. Eighty. There was a big party due to take place that afternoon, hosted by Peg in her brand-new house up on the bench, with its magnificent view of the lake. No one in the family was capable of mentioning that house without also mentioning its magnificent view of the lake, including—especially—Peg. And Art had promised to be there, in fact the last time he visited he promised his sister he'd arrive a couple of days in advance to help with the preparations. Well, surely no one had expected him to keep that particular promise.

Eighty. Art's father had died of a heart attack the year after he retired; he'd been well in the morning, puttering around the garden, then dropped dead in the afternoon on his way to take a nap. Every time Art arrived home he still expected to see them both.

Art checked out at the motel reception. The skinny kid behind the desk offered him a weak-looking cup of coffee, which he declined. He'd stop for breakfast and gas in Hope.

He knew how the visit would play out, he'd shown up to enough birthday parties and special occasions to know exactly what was waiting for him. His entrance would cause a fuss: Peg would be happy to see him, but Frank would telegraph his disapproval by asking pointed questions about when he was going to get an office job and settle down. And everyone else would bombard him with questions about where he was working, what he was doing, except no one would say what they were really thinking—they never asked about Rose. They never mentioned Celeste. It was as though they were afraid of how he might respond. The old ladies would flutter and beckon him to come near, and the men would get up off their chairs to slap him on the back. The kids would tug his hands to get his attention, as the women adjusted their skirts and checked their blouses, ran their tongues over their teeth. There'd be at least forty people in the room, his mother's friends, Peg and Frank's friends, the whole of the family—Peg's own family, Eddie and his wife Carol, plus a heaving mass of kids. Everyone would be there, apart from the missing: Tilly. Dad.

And his mother. In her birthday best. She'd find it tricky, she always found it tricky. She'd want to ask him what he was doing, give him advice and counsel him to change his ways, to patch things up with Rose, to . . . But she knew that he didn't want to answer her questions, didn't want her advice, so she'd try, and fail, to land on another subject. And she'd end up saying . . . nothing. Smiling and nodding, standing there a bit stiffly, as if at a formal event. And sometimes she'd get tears in her eyes as she looked at him and he knew she was thinking about him and Rose and the baby. Celeste. And that was too much for Art. If that happened again, he'd have to leave. She'd understand that he'd have to leave.

Might be best not to show up at all.

When Art got as far as Keremeos he realized he had a choice: north toward the birthday party, or south down the new highway to Osoyoos and, from there, into the US. He felt like driving, he always enjoyed driving. He'd recently come off a big contract on the Island and, despite this past lost weekend with Sal in Nanaimo, he had an appetite for more of the same. His next job was lined up and waiting for him the following week, and he needed to relax, to let loose, before heading back to camp. He hadn't managed to buy his mother a present yet; he should get her a present. He'd head down to the US—Spokane. He'd turn up with a present a day or two after the party; she'd have him all to herself that way. They could spend some time. Talk. Really talk. Eddie and his family were bound to be in town for an extra few days; Eddie could talk to Art about the garage, Art could talk to Eddie about the logging company. They'd have a beer or two or three. He'd go see Peg as well; Peg would be calm, the party frenzy passed. She'd be cross with him but she'd forgive him. She always did.

Art had never been to Spokane. When he was a kid they used to think of it as the big metropolis to the south but when he finally arrived—it was further than he thought it would be—he saw it was just a low-rent, down-at-heel town, a former trading post that had peaked in the previous century. Art drove around looking for the biggest, grandest old hotel in honour of his mother's birthday; besides, he figured he'd meet a better class of woman there.

Like the town, the hotel had seen better days. The man on reception made him pay for the night then and there, as though afraid Art would depart once he saw the room. The bar out back—he wasn't sure if it was part of the hotel or not—was a dive, with a flickering neon Pilsner sign that looked about to fall off the wall, and a mirror so rusted and warped it had been a long time since anyone had seen themselves in it. Which was just as well since the clientele was also ugly and worn out. Luckily, Art appreciated a dive as much as the next man and he spent the evening sitting at the bar. Canadians liked to maintain that American beer was so weak you had to drink twice as much of it; Art didn't know if this was true, but he drank twice as much just in case, along with a few bourbon chasers. When he returned from the Gents around midnight, thinking maybe it was time to call it a day, a woman with long blonde hair and the shortest skirt he'd ever seen was perched on his bar stool. He wasn't sure whether or not she was a prostitute but he had plenty of cash so he didn't care much either way. She smiled at him. He put his hand on her thigh up near the hem of her skirt by way of a greeting. Her face went dark and she shouted "Hey!" As though she'd summoned a genie, a man appeared out of nowhere at her side. He was taller than Art by several inches and, Art figured, approximately twice his size. The man drained his glass and then smashed it on the bar. Someone across the room shrieked. The man turned toward Art with the jagged remains, smiling.

Art was not a fighter. Sometimes things got out of hand in camp but more often than not it was over a game of cards, and since Art never played, he stayed clear of trouble. But not today. The enormous man advanced with the broken glass and Art felt a powerful rush of anger, clear and searing. *Stupid fucking asshole. Who the fuck does he think he is?*

Art grabbed the man by the wrist and wrenched the broken glass from him, the shards slicing into the flesh of his palm. And then, without thinking, he drove the glass into the man's arm. The man gasped and fell to his knees, clutching the sleeve of his coat, while the blonde began to scream, backing away as though Art was about to come after her next. The barman turned to reach for the telephone, a look of horror on his face. Art picked up his jacket and departed.

In the bathroom of his hotel room—damp patches on the ceiling, peeling wallpaper—Art did his best to pluck the fragments of glass out of his hand. The cut at the base of his thumb was deep. He could hear sirens. One, two, three vehicles. He held his hand under cold running water until it went numb, wrapped it in a towel and swallowed half a dozen aspirin. He located the keys to his truck, threw everything into his holdall, and left.

Art headed north out of town toward Kettle Falls, but instead of continuing on and crossing at Laurier, he drove along the south side of the Columbia River to Northport, and beyond that, on the back road across the border. There was no border guard there, not even a sign to mark the frontier. Once he was past Trail, he pulled into a rest area. The sun was coming up. The aspirin had worn off and his hand was throbbing. He took a good long drink from the bottle of bourbon he kept in his glovebox, settled down on the bench of his truck with his jacket as a pillow, and went to sleep.

Later that day, as he was parking on Woodruff, his mother came out on the porch. Sixth sense, as always. She was a tall woman, five foot nine—or at least she used to be, having shrunk a bit. She was so thin in her housedress and apron that she looked more like a collection of bones than a woman. Seeing her like this, the day after her eightieth birthday, Art felt a pain run through him. Yesterday all he could think about was how much he didn't want to go to the party; now, as always, he wondered why he'd felt that way.

"Arthur!" she exclaimed as he walked up the steps. "You're here!"

"Mother!" Art replied. "Happy birthday!"

He'd stopped to buy her a bunch of flowers in town, and now he mouthed the words as she said them, the words she never failed to repeat: "I've never understood why people cut flowers when they look so much nicer in the garden."

"It's March, Mother," Art replied. "There are no flowers in any gardens anywhere around here." As always when he visited, he wondered how his mother managed to inspire in him this unwelcome combination of love and aggravation.

She nodded. He knew she was pleased.

"Tilly loved flowers," she said.

"She did," Art nodded. Tilly. The dead felt as present as the living here. "I'm sorry I missed the party."

She waved her hand as though to dismiss all that. He followed her through the house into the kitchen. It had become the house of someone who lived alone, which Art found discomfiting; all that was left of his father were his hats beside the front door. His mother's interest in politics had not abated; there was a stack of magazines and newspapers on the side table, next to an orderly pile of clippings, her scissors, and her reading glasses.

"Peg's house is so far out of town," she said. "Why do you need a view of the lake when you drive past it every day regardless?"

Art knew this was her way of saying it was okay that he didn't make it to her party, but of course this made him feel worse. Part of him wished she'd tell him off, berate him, tell him to get his priorities straight.

"And all those windows—it must cost a fortune to heat," she added.

His hand felt as though it was radiating enough heat to keep the whole town warm. He'd been trying to keep it out of sight behind his back since he'd arrived, but she spotted it now.

"Oh, Art," she said, alarmed. "What happened?"

"Cut myself," he said, "changing a tire."

The towel from the hotel bathroom was still wrapped around his hand though the blood had crusted and dried. As they stood together over the bathroom sink, his mother unwrapped the towel gingerly. The worst of the cuts, at the base of his thumb, began to bleed again. She pressed a cotton bandage against it while Art tried unsuccessfully not to wince. He hadn't managed to remove all the glass. He took a deep breath and grasped hold of the sink with his other hand. For a moment, he thought he might pass out.

"You need a stitch, Art," she said, looking at her watch. "The doctor's office is still open. Let's go."

—

A couple of days later, his wound cleaned and stitched, his mother's pot roast and apple pie eaten and appreciated, Art was ready to leave. He'd missed out on seeing Eddie, who'd had to get back to work, to Calgary, the day after the party. Art spent time with Peg and Frank and their family—Peg had four kids now, including a late, unexpected arrival, a little girl who was ten years younger than the rest—but the noise and thrum of that household made him feel uneasy. He'd sat with his mother in the evenings but all his resolutions about making it up to her for missing her party hadn't amounted to much. There were too many gaps, too many things too painful to mention, too many people missing. As usual, he couldn't wait to get away.

Instead of heading to the highway, Art drove out along the lake. Even this time of year, when the earth was winter-scorched brown and the orchards bare, the valley was beautiful. The land here was sweeter, the slopes to the lake softer. He rolled down the car window and let the sun warm his face. He drove past the end of the road that ran through Rose's property, the turning so familiar he had to fight the urge to steer his car into it. Once beyond it, he pulled over to the side of the street and climbed out. He took a deep breath and filled his lungs with air—the same air Rose must be breathing right now.

After Celeste had gone, he'd signed on for a short contract logging on the coast, then another, longer contract, then a permanent job. He fell back into his old ways, longer shifts for more hours than anyone else. He started drinking even more heavily, and when he did go home, he got into a bad habit of turning up drunk. And Rose seemed to need Art, want Art, less than ever. It became easier to stay away. And that was it: it was over between them. There was no formal declaration, no falling out, no ultimatums. Instead a gradual going, going, then gone. One day when he turned up in her yard she greeted him with an envelope. He opened it in front of her: divorce papers.

He was still in love with her, that would never change. But there was no way back to what they'd once had.

As he stood by the side of the road that led to Rose, knowing she was most likely working on her land nearby, he felt it again, the scale of what he'd lost, the gaping hole where his heart once beat.

1977: Naden Harbour

WHEN ART SET OUT across Naden Harbour, the sun was burning off the fog. The enormous bay was well protected by a circle of hills tucked in by clouds: now you see me, now you don't. It was summer, not that you'd know it up here. He was out on the water in the dozer boat with his pike pole, linking boom sticks together to form an enormous bag of logs that he'd later tow across the bay.

He mostly worked on his own these days, which was how he liked it. He'd aged out of the forest and moved onto the water a few years back. But first he'd worked everywhere, for every company in the province—outfits out of Lillooet, Nelson, Gold Bridge, Prince George, Fort St. John, Cranbrook, Kamloops, Prince Rupert, Port Hardy, Port Alberni, Bella Coola, Chemainus, Crofton, Cowichan, Pemberton. Up and down the land. He'd been the oldest high rigger in the company. If you'd asked him a decade ago how he'd feel about leaving the forest, he would have thought it'd be a great loss—but instead he found that on the water, away from the whine and stink of chainsaws and trucks and the splinter and crack of falling trees, he could work at his own pace. He could drink at his own pace as well. Mind his own business. And nurse his head: his head required careful calibration. He needed to drink enough to keep the shakes at bay, but not enough to make him sloppy. Hard liquor only: it was what you drank in camp, especially on the Charlottes, which were so remote you had to travel to work by floatplane. Twelve bottles of Scotch in your kit went a lot further than twelve bottles of beer.

He didn't have a lot of credit left in the bank of good will with his current boss, a new fellow, sent over from head office in Vancouver. Art had missed the floatplane out of Prince Rupert after his last break away from camp, and the guy was determined to hold it against him. Art needed to stay in his good books. But out on the water there was no one watching, no one keeping track of anything other than the logs themselves, where they were and where they needed to be. And *that* he could do, and beautifully. Bag the logs, drag the whole lot of them across the bay. Back to camp in time to eat. Sleep. Get up and do it all over again. He still worked more efficiently than anyone else. In the booming grounds down south he used to be known for how he could skip across the unstable log boom as though it was a dance floor—the Fred Astaire of logging. So for the most part they left him to it.

Today was a good day: he was on his own and it was not raining. Not that he minded the rain any longer; up here, if you minded the rain you'd go crazy. Up in the camp there was an old copy of *National Geographic* that stated that in the archipelago of the Queen Charlotte Islands it rains, on average, three hundred and twenty-five days of the year.

Art set his course. His destination was near the top end of the bay, behind a spit, where half a dozen bags of logs were chained together and waiting to be loaded onto the enormous empty barge floating nearby, black and sinister-looking, its rusted cranes arched like huge claws, ready to grab whatever came near. The load Art was towing was so damn heavy his progress would be slow—eight hours or so given the tide.

Art fetched his binoculars. He'd bought a bird book a few years back and he kept it stashed on the boat next to his old canteen. At the north end of the bay, in the Alexandra Narrows, out near Virago Sound, he could see a small knot of fishing boats and, in their midst, a huge crowd of gulls and rhinoceros auklets—seabirds that looked like puffins, but with little white horns protruding from their orange bills—diving and swooping and making a tremendous racket. He was far more fond of the birds than he was of the fishermen, who were forever encroaching on his territory. Right now, fishermen and birds alike were preying on a fish ball, the birds after the needlefish while the fishermen tried to catch whatever was below the surface herding the fish into the scrum. They were likely hoping for salmon, though it could be seals. Maybe a whale. Moments later the birds scattered as though they were partying teenagers whose parents had come home early. The fishing boats puttered off. Sun broke through the cloud cover and glinted on the water.

The name Naden Harbour was a leftover from a more optimistic past—no one lived on the bay, as far as Art knew, nor anywhere near it. There'd been a whaling station here once upon a time, but all that remained of it was a ruined cement dock. Anthropologists figured the islands once had a population of over ten thousand people, but smallpox and war had reduced the Haida population to about three hundred and fifty by the beginning of the twentieth century, gathered together in Old Masset and Skidegate. There was an abandoned village near the narrows, rotting totems, cedar longhouses collapsing into the dense undergrowth. Art found the totem poles frightening, though he wasn't quite sure why. They had a power and mystery that alarmed him—animals with human faces, big eyes staring out at the world, carrying messages he couldn't decode. He remembered a time when he was scared of the ocean as well, back during his first job on the coast, nervous of the swell and the tide, the feeling of menace the fog brought with it, the mist resting heavily on the water, obscuring the land, the wind whipping his face. It gave him the sense of being in a different world, that his charts might not be accurate—how could they be accurate, when the tide rose and fell so dramatically, when the Pacific rushed up onto the rocky shoreline and into the trees?

The trees here were bigger than any other trees Art had ever seen, they were taller than the tallest building in Vancouver, a single branch had more life to it than any tree you'd see in the interior of the province where the scrawny pines fought the stunted firs for water and sunshine. In the Charlottes you'd stand up to your eyebrows in salal and god-knows-what foliage and you'd feel as though if you were still for a moment too long it would claim you, the land would pull you in and root you there, and you'd become part of it and your flesh would turn to moss, your hair would sprout fiddleheads and you'd find huckleberries where you once had balls. And soon enough not even your friend who had come looking for you would be able to spot you, his eyes would sweep over you, over your many shades of green, and truth be told, you wouldn't mind. You'd want to stay there, rooted, breathing the rainforest air. The earth's pre-history, the forest primeval. Art half expected to see a dinosaur emerge. He left everything behind when he was in those trees, out on that water, nothing he'd done in his life mattered, nothing meant anything. He felt a kind of stillness. A kind of quiet.

Despite the heavy load he was making good progress, and the day began to melt away. He fetched a sandwich and looked through his binoculars while he chewed. He spotted a couple of boats up ahead. Cabin cruisers. Tourists. That was unusual. They were already through the narrows, and they were heading in his direction. Two boats, two couples. The women stationed in the prow of each boat, on the lookout for deadheads. The stray logs rested below the surface of the water like alligators, and they'd puncture your hull if you weren't careful. The tourists kept coming toward him, as though they'd gotten it into their own deadheads that they should be sociable, out there on the water with no one else to bother. Idiots.

When they were less than half a mile away, Art stepped out of the tug's cabin. "Get back," he shouted, "get the hell back." They clearly had no idea how difficult it was for him to stop when towing a bag this size, and he wasn't about to slow down for them. He waved his arms over his head and shouted again, and as he waved he felt a bit dizzy. Maybe he'd had a little too much to drink already. Art watched as one of the women used an oar to push a deadhead away, but the logs were massive and unwieldy. The last thing he needed on his watch was some accident involving tourists.

The boat in the lead killed its engine, and the other followed suit. They paused for a moment, then they started up again, looping around and heading out of Naden Harbour. Out of Art's territory. But as the boats grew smaller, Art felt a kind of loneliness seep into his bones. He wasn't fit for company. He didn't like to think about how he must smell—pitch and bark, cigarettes, sea salt, fish guts and sweat and, beneath that, today's bourbon, yesterday's whiskey. He'd given up his social life years ago now, he'd even stopped seeking out the company of women. But sometimes, some afternoons out on the water, he felt lonely.

He hadn't been home for more than five years. Not since his mother died. Peg had tracked him down through the union; the rep had found him in the bar in Masset and Art had given the guy a black eye for his effort. It was as though the incident years ago in Spokane had marked him in some way—nowadays he was forever getting into bust-ups in bars, a night out on the town wasn't really a night out without giving or receiving a black eye, and his nose had been broken so many times it looked like a bulbous mushroom. He thought the union man had been insulting his mother, not delivering a piece of bad news.

He'd made it to the funeral on time. The rep arranged it all—a flight south first thing in the morning, a rental car for him to pick up at the airport. Art turned up at Peg's house that evening with a bouquet of flowers and a bottle of whiskey. When Peg opened the door to him he was grateful for the look of relief on her face.

"I hope Frank has a suit he can lend me?" he said.

Art still didn't like Frank. The pair of them, in their big house up on the bench with that magnificent view of the lake. Four kids and two cars. A proper office man, in a suit and tie, with his university degree. Last Art heard, and this was years ago, Frank had scaled the heights of the teaching profession, climbed all the way up to Superintendent of Schools—the job title made Art laugh, as though Frank was now a bureaucratic version of a comic book superhero. Frank was a catch, at least that's what Peg said, which annoyed Art no end—it was Frank who was lucky to have Peg. Art still wondered what had happened to his once-fearless sister, the girl who had run at Mister Theodore brandishing a stick. She'd been the brave one, always. But then he remembered: nothing happened to her. It was him the thing had happened to, it was him who had caused it all.

The night before his mother's funeral, Art had lain in bed, unable to sleep. He'd been relegated to a fold-out cot in a corner of the rec room. Rain moved in across the hills and he could hear it hitting the tarp on the hot tub Frank had installed a couple of years earlier. Back in camp Art had a room to himself, a glorified storeroom attached to the cook-house, raw drywall and plywood, rough beams. He kept his booze supply under his bed, behind his kit bag, and that night he'd stashed a bottle from Peg's drinks trolley inside one of his boots. He thought about his sister, tucked up in her bed in the master bedroom with its big ensuite, Frank snoring at her side. He wondered if she was listening to the rain and the immense silence of the land, out there beyond the town with its shopping malls and car showrooms.

There was a big crowd at the funeral. Art had been to too many funerals in this place; there'd been too many radio calls to the camp to tell him someone had died. He sat between Eddie and Peg, Eddie stricken and unable to speak, Peg stiff but stoic in her best dark skirt-suit. He put his arm around his sister and she softened and leaned into him. They both drew a deep breath. Once. Twice. Art knew he could not be relied upon in any way, shape or form, but the fact was that Peg didn't rely on him, she hadn't had to rely on him for decades. No one did. And that, Art thought, was a good thing.

They'd buried Celeste in the Catholic cemetery on the

other side of town; Art hated to think of her there, by herself. Art had built an arbour on Rose's land in her honour; he'd carved Celeste's name into a wooden bench he made by hand. He hoped it was still there, the climbing roses he'd planted full and healthy.

Rose wasn't at the funeral. He'd heard a while back that she'd got married again—a lawyer. According to Peg, he was a Toronto man who wore expensive city suits that fit him perfectly but made him look uncomfortable at the same time, as though he'd have liked nothing better than to roll up his sleeves and kick back with a cold beer. But still a white-collar man, like Frank. They'd built a new house above the lake, and Peg told Art they divided their time between the valley and Vancouver, where they had another house.

They headed up to Peg's after the service, where a huge spread seemed to Art to have miraculously appeared—all of his mother's favourite dishes lined up on the dining room table, right down to the devilled eggs. Nancy was bustling around the kitchen as though she owned it. She was wearing a belted black dress that was a little too short for the occasion.

"Nancy," Art said, "you look like a million bucks."

"Thank you," she replied, blushing.

"She makes me feel like an old housewife," said Peg.

"You are an old housewife, Peg," Nancy said. "You and me both. Doesn't mean we can't make an effort." And she slapped herself on the bottom for emphasis.

"Wait a minute. If anyone is slapping butts around here, it should be me," Art said. And he turned to Peg expecting her to laugh, but instead she looked appalled.

Nancy straightened her dress. "She was a great girl, your mother. Much loved in the town."

"Where's that husband of yours?" Art asked.

"Stomach bug," she said brightly, "he felt so bad he couldn't be here. He loved your mum."

"I never understood why you married a wop," Art said.

"Jeez, Art," said Peg.

"I'm sorry," Art said, "not used to polite company."

"Oh, Artie," Nancy laughed, "you wag." She ground out her cigarette.

Peg looked furious. Art wasn't sure what had made her angrier—his comment, or the flirting. She handed him a big platter of baked ham that Frank had carved earlier. "Take that through, will you? There's space in the middle of the table."

The wake went on through the afternoon and into the evening, people coming and going, food eaten, drinks poured, drinks topped up again. By around eleven, most people had departed, the kids gone to bed. Frank lit a fire in the big stone fireplace and gently directed Peg to an armchair. "You've been on your feet all day," he said. Despite the service and the great crowd, they'd somehow managed to go the whole day without mentioning their mother, without talking about how much they loved her.

Art sat down on the sofa, so soft it threatened to swallow you up if you weren't careful, and Nancy came and sat beside him, the sofa rolling them together. Rusty the dog appeared from wherever she'd been hiding and settled down at Peg's feet.

"Rusty must be ancient," Art said. "The oldest spaniel in the world."

"Rusty the Second," Frank said.

"Rusty the Third," Peg corrected.

"Pass me your bourbon," Nancy replied. Nancy's thigh was touching Art's, and after a while he felt as though his leg was burning, his body was burning, such was the heat that Nancy was generating. They sat like this for a long time. Every once in a while, Frank rose and poked the fire, and Rusty the Third sighed with contentment. Nancy moved against him closer still.

Later, when Frank was snoring and Peg looked as though she'd nodded off as well, Nancy stood up, stretched her back, and made her way to the stairs that led down to the basement. She paused there, and looked back at Art. Then she went down the stairs. Moments later, Art followed.

She was waiting in the half-light at the bottom of the stairs. When he caught up with her, she took his hand. "Come on, Artie," she said, though he didn't need convincing. They went into the furnace room and shut the door.

In a way Art was surprised it hadn't happened before, back when they were young. His whole life he'd had an easy time with women: he liked them, they liked him. Up and down the province, there were women he could call on weekends between shifts. And if the women hung up at the sound of his voice, he only had to find the right bar at the right time.

Though lately, truth be told, it had become a little more difficult. He'd never been opposed to paying for sex, but these days he had to pay for it more often than not.

But not tonight. Nancy.

Nancy gasped when Art pushed inside her and he covered her mouth with one hand to keep her quiet. They paused like that a moment, her legs wrapped around him, her back against the door. Around them, the house was silent. Art thought for a moment he could hear talking, but it was only the furnace ticking as it cooled off.

Nancy left the room first, walking purposefully. Peg and Frank had both woken up and begun another round of clearing up. When Art stepped into the kitchen Peg gave him a look of reproach. "What are you up to, Art?" she asked. He didn't reply. He could see she knew what he had done. He could see she knew everything there was to know about him—she always had, she always would.

Art hated himself a little, once again. He wished he'd stayed away—though that really would have been unforgivable. He longed to be up north in the endless trees, pressed between the cold forest green and the black grasping sea, remote from the world of family and friends, remote from the world of small towns strung out across the province like beads on a broken necklace.

The two tourist boats were distant now, at the top of the narrows at the far end of the bay. Art thought about the time he'd taken a skiff across to the north side of Naden Harbour in order to get a better look at the abandoned Haida village. The surrounding forest was a little more open than the rest, the ground a spongy mass of fern and moss, fallen cedar and hemlock. Everything had been green and slippery, rich and moist and mushroomy and—what was that word?—verdant. Like a big green lung. He'd come across what looked like three short, fat, featureless totem poles planted cheek-to-cheek, and had realized they must have been mortuary poles, like those he'd read about in *National Geographic*. The bentwood boxes they once would have housed were long since removed to museums, the human remains still tucked up inside. The creeping fear that he sometimes felt on these islands grew stronger—he felt like he was trespassing. He probably was trespassing. He heard a snap, like someone had stepped on a fallen branch, and spun round. *Mister Theodore*? He gave himself a shake and headed back down to the beach.

1989: Money

ART DIDN'T RETIRE FROM LOGGING. He had never considered retiring—he'd planned to keep on working and living the life for as long as earthly possible. Instead, he stopped getting hired. All the gyppo firms he'd worked for over the years had been sold or amalgamated and the new management eased him out or plain turned him away. No more contracts. No more paydays.

He'd gotten old somehow, that was the problem. He'd done every job there was to do, from captaining the boats in the booming grounds to rigging at the top of the trees. He'd cut down more trees than he'd smoked cigarettes. Once he had a reputation for doing longer contracts for rougher work in worse conditions than anyone else. But these days if he had a reputation it was not for his work ethic.

Over the years logging had become political. People had opinions now. Up and down the province, people who knew nothing about logging felt the need to pontificate; there were protests and blockades. Art was never all that interested in trees for trees' sake. He thought of them as a resource to be taken from the land, always there, infinite. His parents had settled in this far-flung corner of the empire only yesterday, and their ancestors had taken the land from the Indigenous people and the land was what gave them their living. They didn't think twice. Art's task was to take the trees down and reduce them to logs. From there, they'd be turned into plywood. Two-by-fours. Sawdust. Nothing left of the forest in the tree. The whole province a patchwork, as though it'd been scalped by a no-good barber who kept cutting off more hair in the hope of fixing his mistakes. And Art was fine with that. But on the Charlottes it felt different, even to Art. The Charlottes weren't like other places. When you felled one of those trees, you were bringing hundreds of years of living to an end. When you cut down one of those trees—that was it, that tree was gone. And it turned out that those trees, well, those trees were not infinite. That got to Art a little at the end, he'd admit it.

Yet the land had extracted its vengeance too. That kid boss—the last one who'd fired him—was right: he was drinking more. He got the shakes in the morning, every morning, which was easy enough to deal with—all he needed to do was have a drink. But he had blackouts now, in the evening—that never used to happen.

During that last year of working, he'd head up the Sunshine Coast to Gibson's on his downtime to stay with Gilly Evans.

She was a schoolteacher he'd met at a free outdoor concert he'd stumbled upon the summer before. Nice woman, bit of a hippie, with grown-up children, used to living her own life in her own way, and with her Art had glimpsed the possibility of another future. Hauling logs for Gilly's woodpile instead of the company. Mowing the lawn and fixing the lousy plumbing in her little house with its view of the water that would rival even Peg's. But Gilly had cottoned on to the drinking pretty quickly—fact was, Art never tried to hide it, there was no point—and on one of his visits she went so far as to suggest he had a problem and that maybe he should go to a meeting.

"The union?" he'd said.

"No, you great eejit," she replied, "AA."

"Oh, you mean the Automobile Association," he said, but he knew what she meant.

She sighed and put her hands on her hips; he went in for a kiss, and she relented.

But it turned out she was serious. She said he'd either deal with it or she'd close the door on him. She closed the door. He went back to work.

And then a couple of months after that, he was working with a small crew in the booming ground, Howe Sound, when he slipped up. It was pissing rain and the fog was thick above the water, and the gulls were making a racket—Art could hear them, but couldn't see them, and he had wondered what had gotten them riled. He steered the sidewinder alongside the log boom; he'd done this manoeuvre so many times he could almost do it in his sleep—he could do it drunk, sick, exhausted after weeks on the job without a break. He could move that boat through the water like other people buttered bread.

He'd seen a lot of accidents in his time. He was there when Len Cutler was crushed by that enormous tree on the ridge above the Yakoun Valley on the Charlottes—a tree so big they'd left it 'til the clear-cut was nearly complete. They were on a new road that had been put in a few weeks before, the smell of the felled forest all around them, moss and ferns and churned-up mud, along with the acrid tang of chainsaws and of the diesel smudging the sky. They'd been working on this tree for a couple of hours, first on the undercut, then placing the falling wedges into position one at a time. They paused, nearly ready to pull it down, and for a moment, everything was quiet. Art stared up at the tree, thinking it was a thing of massive beauty. How a tree could get so big was beyond his reckoning. Hundreds of years old. Then the foreman shouted in alarm and, before they realized what was happening, the butt kicked out and smashed into Len like a full-speed train. As the tree came away it made a sound so loud that it seemed to blot out all life for that moment, an end of the world sound. It crushed Len like a bug before it crashed down the mountainside like a skyscraper going head over heels. Len lay there, dead on the ground in the mud and the dirt, his head smashed, everything else smashed with it, and Art was overcome by uncontrollable vomiting, wave after wave, 'til he thought he'd have no guts left.

And that day on the water, the gulls were making a racket, and Art wondered why, and he looked up, into the fog, and his foot went down off the side of the boat, where there should have been tight-packed logs, and he fell in, slipped in like a fish poured straight from a bucket and into the drink. He opened his eyes in the cold salty seawater, felt his clothes and his boots fill, and watched as the gap in the logs closed up above him. He thought about Celeste. And he thought, okay. All right.

Jared McGill, a clueless teenager from Prince George who kept losing all his money in the poker games in camp, ran along the log boom, pushed the logs apart, reached down between them, and pulled Art up and out with the strength that only comes from blind panic and extreme youth.

"Were you drinking on the job?" his boss asked later that day, when Art had dried out and was sitting in the harbour office with a cup of tea. He was a young guy, Art figured less than half his age, who wore a suit and tie to the harbour office every day as though he was working in some other cleaner, brighter, less brutal industry.

Art couldn't remember the last time he hadn't been drinking on the job. But it had never stopped him from getting the work done. He smiled and said, "What was your name again?"

And that was that. He was finished, on the floatplane south for the last time.

Now no one would hire him. His hands weren't nearly as capable as they'd once been. The tendon he'd severed all those years ago in Spokane ached—sometimes the whole hand was numb, almost useless. And over the years he'd dislocated his shoulder so many times on the job that he'd learned to fix it by sticking a tennis ball in his armpit and slamming himself against the nearest tree. One time he couldn't find a ball and used an apple from his lunch bag instead—messy, but it worked. But it was the thumb that was giving him the most grief currently: how could something so minor hurt so much?

Art wasn't ready to retire. Over the past decade he had invested in a couple of businesses, but nothing ever worked out. There'd been a patent on a chainsaw one of his pals had developed that had failed, and a truck logging outfit that had crashed and burned, literally. Too many of his business contacts were former loggers themselves who hadn't a clue about the world beyond cutting down trees. So Art had tried to diversify, to stop investing in anything to do with logging. He put money into a construction project in Vancouver, a new luxury hotel to be built on the water near Stanley Park. He'd attended a presentation in a fancy suite and been impressed by the blueprints, the table-sized model with its tiny couples walking hand in hand between tiny trees, along a tiny boardwalk. But the backers had gone south into the US, taking his money along with that of a number of other investors. The project turned out to have been an elaborate con; they didn't even own the land they were pretending they were going to build on. Art was well and truly ripped off, and there was nothing he could do about it.

The hotel project was his first real financial loss. He didn't go to the police, worried that some of the blame for the failed scheme would somehow rub off on him. It turned out that what Rose had said to him years ago was still true—he was no good with money.

Now Art was unemployed, and he needed money fast. He had one last paycheque in the bank, from his last big contract, and he knew it was his final chance to get in on the ground with something big. He'd met a woman called Sheila who lived in Hope, and he shacked up with her in her little house. It was so decrepit there was a foot-wide gap between the porch and the front door that Art kept meaning to fix. Sheila was a drinker as well. "We're made for each other," she said one night as they staggered home from the bar. Art wasn't so sure.

And then he ran into Bob Nestor at the country fair in Cloverdale; Art had been driving to nowhere in particular and stopped to buy something to eat at the salt beef stand. He hadn't seen Nestor for years. And it turned out Nestor had started a commercial nursery—tulips and roses—on the agricultural land reserve in Surrey. He was keen to show it off to Art, so they drove over to take a look that afternoon. Nestor and his business partner, Ranj Singh, had purchased a big piece of farmland that had been used to grow soft fruit and corn, and they were converting the land from crops to flowers. Rows of new greenhouses glinted in the distance.

"All very high-tech," Nestor said, "irrigated, lit, heated, ventilated. You name it. It's an all-year-round operation. Not weather-dependent."

"Where's your market?" Art asked.

"Vancouver. Hotels, restaurants, high-end florists. There's so much money in that town now. Seattle as well, we hope, in the not-too-distant future. Once we've made our name."

Art thought about his hotel that wasn't a hotel. Since he'd been conned a hotel had actually gone up on that land, five stars and fifteen storeys. They probably had a large budget for floral displays.

"Ranj has been in nurseries his whole life—his brother has a nursery over in Abbotsford. He knows the business inside out. I'm the finance guy."

Art laughed, but Nestor was serious. "I've been to night school, Art! I'm a qualified accountant."

"Really?"

"Well," Nestor said, "almost. Just a few credits short."

"Where's Ranj from?" Art asked.

"Here," Nestor replied. "Surrey."

"No, you know . . ."

"Oh," Nestor said. He waved his hand, "India. Punjabi. I don't know. Does it matter?"

Art shrugged. It probably didn't matter. People came from all over the place these days. He looked at the rows of greenhouses, and beyond that, the sunflowers, their big faces turned toward the sun.

"We'll have this business up and running in no time. Investors are lining up," Nestor said. "Any interest?"

Nestor seemed nervous, and this made Art uneasy. But he was an old friend. He'd witnessed Art's marriage to Rose. He was excited about the business. It was a good opportunity.

A couple of weeks later, Art received a contract in the mail at Sheila's and went down to the bank to transfer the money.

Nestor called to thank him. "Listen Art, leave us to it."

"What do you mean?"

"You're an investor, not a partner. You would have needed to put in more money to be a partner."

"I wasn't planning on coming down to help with the pruning."

"Good," Nestor said, laughing.

Art hung up the phone and that feeling of unease returned. But Sheila fixed him a rye and seven and it passed, like everything.

Eventually, Nestor did invite Art down to come try out the goods, and Art turned up expecting to be given a bunch of tulips. There were tulips all right, in every colour under the sun, but it turned out they were a cover. Out beyond the greenhouses there was an underground bunker, built during the war though no one was sure why, and Nestor was using it to grow cannabis. He was upfront about the new focus of the business. "No point in hiding it," he said, "the profits are going to be huge. BC bud. Americans are crazy for it." Not only that, but Nestor had set up a brothel in the property's battered old ranch house. If the authorities ever asked, Nestor said he'd tell them he was providing accommodation for the migrant farm workers the nursery trade relied on—a tidy answer because it was also true. It turned out the ladies were more lucrative than the tulips, but of course nothing was as lucrative as the dope.

Nestor escorted Art into the rec room of the ranch house, where tulip bulbs were drying on the bar-top alongside empties. The ladies filed in so that, Nestor said, Art could "inspect" them. Ten girls. They were a sad collection of mostly Indian women who looked drugged-out and under-age.

"Investors' privileges," Nestor said, smiling.

Art found himself wondering where the girls came from, maybe one of the bands up the coast, maybe they were Haida or Tlingit who'd come south looking for work and somehow ended up here.

"Sheila's expecting me," Art said, though he'd told Sheila he might be gone the night.

"You'll be seeing big returns on your investment in no time," Nestor said.

"Good," said Art. He got in his truck and drove away.

A month later, and it was all over the papers. Nestor had been bad at the business of cooking the books, despite his night-school training. He and his partner were arrested and charged with racketeering and smuggling and soliciting and distributing, you name it.

Art was shocked. Not just because he'd lost his savings. He'd lived a rough old boy's life, but Bob Nestor running those women—well, that'd been too much and he'd known it. Those girls looked sad and sick and very young. He should have gone to the police. But he'd felt too far gone with the investment, he couldn't risk losing all his savings again, not when he had no possibility of finding work. But now he'd lost everything anyway. He realized in hindsight that Nestor probably knew it when he asked him for money—knew Art was too far gone in general to do anything much at all. There for the taking.

Art figured he was lucky they hadn't traced any of the finances back to him. Yet.

Now Art was living in his clapped-out old car in Hope. Sheila had kicked him out. He'd pawned everything he'd ever owned, which hadn't been much to begin with, and he'd had to sell the truck. Every month, as soon as he claimed his pension, he'd end up at the liquor store. Park bench during the day, back to the car at night, moving it to a different part of town from time to time so as to not attract suspicion.

At night when he was trying to get to sleep on the back seat in his old army-issue sleeping bag, his thoughts drifted toward Rose and Celeste. The baby sleeping in her cot, Rose turning toward him in bed. Occasionally when he thought about Celeste he remembered the child that Signora Lavelli had lost. Signora Lavelli in her cellar, surrounded by what was left of her life. He hadn't understood the magnitude of that loss back then. But she'd survived. She'd rebuilt what she could of her life, and carried on. Art had survived the death of Celeste, but as he lay there on the back seat with a bottle of cheap booze, he also knew that he had not.

Art left Hope and drove down to Vancouver. He'd never cared for Vancouver, it was too big, too busy, too full of people who thought they knew best, who would put everyone in the rest of the province—people in logging and fishing and mining—out of work, given half a chance. But he needed work. Once in the city, he had the brilliant idea of looking up Jed Giffen, who he knew from his days in Gold Bridge. Everyone used to call Jed "Harry Truman" on account of the little round glasses he wore; there weren't a lot of spectacle-wearers in the woods. He was a Vancouver lad and had returned to the city once he'd figured out logging wasn't his vocation—and Art had heard he'd done well for himself there.

Turned out Jed was opening a bar in New Westminster with his son. Art drove out to see the place, past East Hastings Street, past the shoals of addicts, the homeless, the laid off and let go. The bar was going to be on the site of an old diner—Jed was adding on a brand-new kitchen twice the size of the old one, as well as a big patio deck that made the most of the view of the river. Jed made Art an offer he couldn't refuse—he could get in on the ground floor if he invested ten grand, and, better still, once the bar was open, Jed would give him a job serving beer. Art felt none of the misgivings he'd had with Nestor. This was a solid investment.

All he needed was the money.

Ten grand.

A few years back he could have had his hands on that—in cash—in a heartbeat.

Where could he get ten grand?

—

The summer traffic was heavy and slow, the road cluttered with people pulling trailers and boats and driving those RVs that seemed to get more enormous with every passing year. But Art didn't mind all that much; he wasn't in a hurry. Besides, he loved the drive across the south of the province, especially once he dropped down off the Crowsnest into the Keremeos Valley and the fruit stands started to pop up along the road.

At Keremeos he stopped to get out of the car and stretch; his shoulder was giving him grief this morning. He crossed the junction on foot, the crossroads where he needed to decide whether to drive north up to the lake to see his sister or south to Osoyoos and maybe on into the USA. Not that turning south was a real option; he hadn't been to the States since that time in Spokane. He didn't know if he could get into, or back out of, the US without being arrested, and he wasn't about to try.

Keremeos was one of those towns that hadn't fulfilled its promise, like so many places in the interior of the province that didn't have enough people to thrive. The only city that felt like it was growing these days was Vancouver. Not that Art had any kind of expertise in these matters. He got back into the car and drove north.

He had the windows rolled down and was working on his driver's tan, one hand on the steering wheel, the other dangling in the sun. There was only a thimbleful of gas left in the tank, so when he turned into the top of the drive, he put the car in neutral and hoped there was enough momentum to carry him through the old cherry orchard to the house.

As always, Peg and Frank's house looked great. Art wondered what it was like to live surrounded by such profusion. Flowers, trees, everything neat and colour-coordinated, plotted, planted and cultivated. Art rolled to a stop behind Peg's car, or what he guessed was Peg's car, a little blue tin can on wheels, and next to it a boat on its trailer. He put his cigarette out carefully in the car's ashtray; the tinder-dryness of the land here was alarming, especially compared to the coast where even the warmest of summers didn't dry the place out. He slammed the car door shut behind him; he didn't want to feel like he was sneaking up on folks. No sign of Peg in the window of the kitchen. He rang the bell, listening for movement from within the house and hearing nothing. He wondered if they were away, and whether or not they kept a key hidden by the front door. He knew Peg wouldn't mind if he moved in while they were gone; Frank he was less sure about. He walked round the house to the back deck where Peg's magnificent view of the lake was laid out in all its glory. The lawn was so green Art could hear the sprinklers even though they weren't running. New gas barbeque, its cover off—maybe they weren't away.

And then he spotted her. Peg was a hundred yards down the slope, where they'd built a kind of pergola. She was lying on a large sun lounger in her bathing suit, a book spread open on her stomach, clearly sound asleep. Rusty the cocker spaniel was sleeping in the shade beneath the lounger. Rusty the Third? Anyway, the dog must be old now, Art thought. Old and deaf.

His lovely sister. He hoped she'd forgiven him, though he couldn't remember what he needed to be forgiven for. Was he in the doghouse? Only one way to find out. He strode across the lawn toward her.

Art sat at the kitchen counter while Peg made sandwiches with tomatoes from the garden. She was talking about her kids, the three oldest who had their own kids, six in total, and the youngest, Kathy, who had finally left home and was studying in England.

"Frank and I are going over in the spring. We've got a great trip planned—London, Bath and Cambridge—and then a week in Italy on the Amalfi coast. We've got it all booked. We were going to go on one of those tours, Globus or something, but then Louie"—at this Peg looked momentarily stricken, but she recovered—"well, he helped Frank figure out how to travel across Europe on the train, he's going to book it for us, you can phone and book if you speak Italian, and where to stay and what to see—his brother owns a hotel"—and now Peg was babbling.

Art thought he'd better interrupt her, put her out of her misery. "I went to all those places during the war."

"Right. Of course you did." Art had told her about the time he'd visited their mother's sister, Aunt Barbara, in England during his first furlough overseas, before he'd been stationed in Italy. He'd told Peg that story a number of times, though it wasn't a story either of them enjoyed all that much. He knew Peg had thought he'd been exaggerating what he'd seen—he painted a picture of abject poverty, as though their aunt was living in a kind of feudal squalor from which there was no escape, though of course their parents had in fact escaped. Could it have really been as bad as that? Or was his memory tricking him, getting mixed up with his stories about the visit until he couldn't quite remember what he'd seen and what he'd told people he'd seen?

After lunch, he and Peg played cribbage on the old board he'd made—he'd spent hours as a kid hammering out the rows of holes with a nail, carving in the lines and markings with his father's penknife, using matchsticks instead of pegs— and she beat him, as always. Art wondered when would be a good time to suggest they have another drink; the beer with lunch hadn't gone very far, and he'd emptied his last bottle of Scotch on the drive that morning.

Art heard Frank's car coming down the drive. He got up from the table and went out through the side door to greet him. As he stepped out of the cool kitchen, he was hit by a wall of heat. He could hear the engine of Frank's old red Chevy wheezing. It occurred to him that he and Frank might be able to talk through the loan without involving Peg. Man to man. Keep Peg out of it—he didn't want her to worry. He didn't want her to know he needed money. But he had no idea how to engineer such a conversation.

Frank was peering at him through the windshield as though not entirely sure what he was seeing. Art walked up to the car and pulled the door open. "Frank!" he said. "Good to see you."

"Hello, Art," Frank said. "Where's Peg?"

"In the kitchen. She beat me at crib."

"You should know better than to play cards with that woman. Did she take your money?" As he spoke, Frank turned slowly in his seat and shifted his feet out the door one at a time. He paused, as though he needed to gather strength. "Is it hot enough for you?"

"It is. It is indeed."

One hand on the car door, Frank inched forward to the edge of the seat, rocked back and forth a couple of times and then stood with an effortful lurch. Art wondered if he'd been drinking.

"Where've you been?" Art asked.

"Rotary. Rotary lunch. We're working on fundraising for the sports centre. Wheelchair ramps."

"Rotary," said Art. "Sounds fun."

"Well, I pay my dues, so I go to the lunch. Art—" Frank interrupted himself—"would you mind getting my jacket off the back seat? There's a bag of groceries there too."

Frank was walking slowly, his left leg at an odd angle, dragging slightly. He was thinner than he used to be, his shoulders more rounded. His hair was thinner too. When he reached the carport he put one hand on the wall of the house as though he needed the additional support. *What's happened here*, Art wondered, *what's happened to Frank?*

—

After dinner—Art made the pre-dinner drinks himself, which helped, and they had wine with the food—they moved out onto the deck. The sun was setting behind the hill on the other side of the lake.

"Don't sit on those," Frank said as Art walked toward a white ironwork table with a set of four matching chairs, "too damn uncomfortable."

"They're not so bad," Peg said, "as long as you use a cushion."

Frank shook his head and pointed at two big, padded wicker armchairs. He sat down heavily in one and indicated to Art to take the other.

"What about you?" Art turned to ask his sister, but she was already dragging one of the ironwork chairs across the deck to join them.

"They weigh a ton," she said. "But I always wanted a set like this."

They sat in silence. The lights of the town twinkled below. Bats flew overhead.

Frank had poured them both a glass of Scotch before they came outside, but Peg had forgotten her own drink—a glass of Harveys Bristol Cream. She'd told Art she didn't much care for it, but they'd been given a bottle by one of their neighbours and she said she felt obliged to drink it. When Art had asked why, she said she couldn't help it, it didn't seem right to pour it down the sink.

Peg went inside to get her glass. Knowing her, she'd also take some time to tidy up once she was there. Art sank down into the cushions of the armchair and looked out at the lake. The knot of tension twisted in his gut. It was time. Now or never.

Art took a deep breath and knocked back the Scotch. "So. Frank."

His brother-in-law looked at him expectantly. Art wondered where to start.

"What brings you to town?" Frank asked.

It was the fourth time he'd asked that question. Each time Art had replied, "To see you folks, of course." But this time he decided to come right out with it. "Well, Frank, I've come to ask you for a loan."

But Frank didn't seem to be listening. He had his hand deep in his trouser pocket, foraging. He pulled out a small piece of rubber tubing, swimming-pool blue. He held it up as though Art would want to inspect it.

"This is what they put in my leg," he said.

"What?" said Art.

"Arterial bypass. Both legs. Arteries so damned furred up they had to replace them. With this tubing. Here, take a look."

Frank chucked the tube at Art, who caught it. But he didn't really want to touch it. He laid it out flat on the broad arm of the chair.

"Isn't that something?" Frank said.

He wasn't sure what to say. "Well, I'll be damned. Are you okay?"

"Sure," said Frank. "A little bionic now, in fact." He paused, then spoke again. "Smoking."

"What?" said Art.

"Smoking-related."

"Smoking-related," Art repeated. "That's rough. I could do with a smoke."

Frank laughed. "So could I."

Art gripped the arms of the wicker chair. There was a sharp piece on the underside of the right arm. He rubbed his finger against it.

"There's a pack," Frank said, "in the shed. Behind the jars of nails."

"There is?"

Frank nodded. "For emergencies. Like this."

"I'll fetch them," Art said.

"You do that," Frank agreed.

Art walked over to the shed on the far side of the house. Frank's gardening and home improvement HQ, the tools organized, lawnmower tucked beside the grass trimmer, everything in its place. And tucked behind the biggest jar, the pack of smokes, half-empty.

Art went back out to sit with Frank.

"Those are your cigarettes," Frank said. "Nothing to do with me." He tipped his head toward the house.

Art nodded. He lit a cigarette and inhaled deeply.

"So, Frank," Art tried again. "I wanted to talk to you. I wanted to ask you about a loan."

Peg arrived behind him with her drink. "You need a loan, Art?"

I timed that badly, thought Art. Since they were kids Peg seemed to have an uncanny ability to hear everything everyone said.

"Yes," he said. There was no backing out of it now.

"What for?" Peg asked.

Art tipped back his head and looked up at the sky, blew a smoke ring toward the moon.

Peg sighed, got up and fetched a large ashtray. Art knew she'd bring the subject up again but he was happy for her to take her time. He wondered if the whole idea was a big mistake. He hadn't expected to find Frank so diminished. He probably should have come to visit more often. Instead, he'd left it 'til he was desperate. Peg was no idiot; she'd see straight through him. It was likely she already had.

"Give me a drag of that cigarette," Frank said. "Just a puff."

Art couldn't remember the last time he'd shared a cigarette with a man, maybe not since his army days. Frank took a long haul on it and handed it back reluctantly. Art held it for a while and wondered if Frank would notice if he put it out in the ashtray, but then he thought better of it—no money for smokes. Rusty came loping across the grass. The dog was a little lopsided, like Frank.

"Where've you been, old boy?" Frank asked. "Chasing bats?"

"You talking to Rusty," Art said, "or me?"

"What brings you to town, Art?" replied Frank.

The next morning, Art swallowed a couple of codeine he found in the bathroom cabinet to ease the edge off his headache. The night before he'd sat up on his own after Peg and Frank had gone to bed. He'd polished off the Scotch and passed out in an armchair for a while before hauling himself into bed.

In the kitchen, Peg was cooking bacon and eggs and the smell made him queasy. Art knew he should eat, but he wasn't hungry. He was never hungry these days; his guts felt unravelled, stringy. When he did eat, more often than not he ended up puking. He poured himself a cup of coffee and sat down across from Frank.

"So. Art," Peg said. "How much money do you need to borrow?"

Art blew on his coffee and took a sip. He had thought this through carefully on his drive from the coast. He figured twelve thousand dollars would do it. Two to get himself back on his feet, and ten more to get him in on the ground floor of the bar. He figured Peg and Frank would have twelve thousand dollars tucked away; he figured they'd have a lot more than that. They'd have bonds and saving plans and mutual funds and premiums and credit union savings accounts, retirement plans and pension funds. All those things that people who were good with money invested in. He had never talked to Peg about money but Frank had made a good living and they'd never gone anywhere or done anything, at least not as far as Art knew. They'd lived in the same house for decades now, they hadn't expanded it, they hadn't built that pool. They didn't have a place down south. They didn't drink too much, they didn't invest in their friends' lousy businesses. Art bet that Peg had a household budget and that she stuck to it. He knew what he would find if he opened the kitchen cupboards:

drawers full of neatly folded paper bags and re-rolled balls of string. He bet she darned socks on a lightbulb—a burnt-out lightbulb that she had saved for that very purpose—and made her own jam and insisted recipes for re-using leftovers were one of her favourite things. Well, maybe not. But she was careful with money. She knew how to save. They were Depression babies, after all.

But now, faced with Peg's question—how much?—he found he couldn't bring himself to ask. Who was he to waltz in here after all this time? Who was he to ask his sister for a dime, let alone twelve grand?

"And what's it for?" Peg added.

He'd thought this through as well. He knew it probably wasn't such a good idea to tell Peg about the bar. He had a story lined up, and he told it: "I've got a friend on the Island with a salmon-fishing, whale-watching outfit. I'm going to go in with him. Help him expand. Buy a second boat. He's got bookings he needs my help to fulfil."

He felt bad about the lie. But as he spoke, he thought it sounded like a great idea. He could spend his days at sea.

Frank nodded. "That sounds like a winner." He looked at Peg. "We'll sell the speedboat."

"Why?" Art said, alarmed. Perhaps they didn't have the kind of cash he'd imagined they would. He had a vague memory of one of their kids—he wasn't sure which—having run a business that went bust. He didn't really know those kids. He didn't really know any of his nieces and nephews, except Eddie's boy David, who'd come work with him up in the Charlottes for a summer a few years back, after he'd finished high school. Could it be Peg and Frank were hard up?

"We've been thinking about selling it," Frank said.

"You've always had a boat. You two love your boat."

"Too hard for me to get in and out of the damn thing these days. This will give us the kick in the pants we needed."

"Since he had the fall," Peg added.

"What fall?"

"When I was in the hospital having my legs done." Frank reached into his pocket for the piece of blue tubing.

"You showed it to Art last night, Frank," Peg said.

"Okay." And, as though he'd had enough of the conversation, as though it was done and dusted, Frank pushed himself up out of his chair and shuffled down the hall.

"What's going on?" Art said, looking at his sister.

"He had a sort of—episode," she said. "The anaesthesia. Some kind of reaction. Lost his mind for a few days."

"What?"

"Didn't know who I was. Thought he'd been kidnapped. He tried to escape from the hospital the day after the operation. Pulled out all his lines and drips. Didn't get very far—he fell and broke his hip. So, then they had to replace the hip. After that he was delirious for—I don't know—weeks. They kept him tied to the bed, with his leg and hip trussed up. Since then, he forgets things."

"Damn," said Art.

Peg gave him a look that ended the conversation. Frank was coming down the corridor, hitching up his trousers.

"We should get five thousand for the boat and trailer," Peg said, her voice bright. "We'll lend you that, Art. We agreed last night, didn't we, Frank?"

Frank nodded, but Art thought he looked a little unsure of what exactly they were talking about.

"We expect regular visits in lieu of interest payments," Peg said. She fetched her chequebook from behind the phone.

"I can't take a cheque, Peg," Art said, his voice low.

His sister gave him one of her calm, appraising looks. "We'll go down to the bank together this morning."

After breakfast they drove downtown, leaving Frank at home with his feet up, listening to the radio. As they pulled into the parking lot behind the bank, Nancy came around the corner on foot.

"There's Nancy," Peg said.

"I see her," Art replied.

"Oh no, she's seen me now."

Peg opened her door and climbed out of the car.

"Hello, Nancy!" she said, her voice unnaturally high.

Art let out a long breath and got out of the car. Nancy gave him a look—he knew that look, he knew what he looked like these days, like an old dog, a half-starved basset hound, all drooping eyes and hollowed-out jowls, his nose like a dented Christmas bauble.

"Hey, Nancy," he said. "You're looking good." She must

have been to the hairdresser's, he reckoned, and she was wearing a pair of white shorts and a bright pink top like she was twenty-one and not in her sixties. She still had legs.

"Art," Nancy replied coolly. "What brings you to town?"

"Visiting my sister."

"We're running a few errands," Peg said.

"Good to see you," Nancy replied.

Art lifted his baseball cap off his head and tipped it toward her.

The bank was cool and dimly lit. As they stood in the line to see a teller, Art said, "I thought you and Nancy were thick as thieves."

"We were." Peg's voice was tight.

"Oh," said Art. He paused. "Well, that's silly. You shouldn't blame Nancy. That was all my fault."

Peg didn't reply.

"How's Louie?"

"He's fine."

"He and Frank still pals?"

Peg nodded.

"They still go fishing?"

"Not anymore."

Art nodded. Frank's . . . condition. But Peg and Nancy— they'd been great friends.

"Get over it, Peg," he said. "Good friends are valuable." Art wasn't sure why he was dishing out friendship advice, he wasn't exactly qualified.

"Maybe you're right," Peg said.

"I usually am."

Peg laughed.

"Oh, yeah," Art said, "you're the one who's always right. I forgot."

Peg leaned over and punched his arm.

By that afternoon, Art was already on his way north. The urge to get up and leave had overpowered him. He felt the envelope, thick with cash, in the inside pocket of his jacket. Peg had a bank draft made out to him, which he had cashed on the spot.

The car took him as far as the nearest gas station, where he used some of Peg's five thousand dollars to fill up. Next stop: the liquor store. He'd go back down to the coast. At least he had a bit of money to put into the bar now, not the full stake Jed wanted, but enough to secure a job for himself, he hoped. He needed to find a place to live . . . How much would that leave him? He'd never worked in a bar, and the thought of it—all that booze—made him feel a bit light-headed. Maybe investing in a salmon-fishing, whale-watching outfit was a better idea. He was tempted to head north, to Prince Rupert, where there'd be a floatplane waiting to take him across the choppy Hecate Strait over to the Charlottes. The water, the logs, the trucks, the trees. All his life he'd been a logger—but that was over now. And everything he knew, he'd left behind in the booming ground.

Peg and Frank's money was burning a hole in his pocket. It

would pay for one hell of a weekend. No. He'd get back down to the coast. And once the bar was bringing in money, he'd pay Peg back, every red cent. It would all work out. It would be all right.

1995: A Night in the Clink

FLASHING BLUE AND RED LIGHTS.

Soggy cardboard, the metal grid of the doorstep.

Everything hurt. Every damn inch of him.

Lights flashing.

A night in the clink. A night in the clink wasn't such a bad idea. Dry bed. Heating.

"Come on, buddy. There's an ambulance here for you."

Art opened his eyes.

"Come on, old man. What's your name?"

What followed was hard to make sense of.

Delirium. Days of it. Weeks.

When Art eventually came to, he spotted a pair of yellowing feet sticking out from under a sheet. Whose feet? A dead man? *Is there a dead man in bed with me?* Or was it he who was dead? Was he in a mortuary—on a slab beneath a sheet?

The next time he came to he underwent an epic struggle to open his eyes; it was as though they'd been weighted down with pennies. He finally managed to crack one eye, only to have to shut it straightaway—sun was streaming in through a big window, too bright.

When he woke again he found that he was surrounded by machines, beeping and humming. He tried to sit up, only to discover he was attached to these machines, rigged and guy-wired.

One night he woke to a dark room. He was as wide awake as he'd ever been, and he felt sure his father was standing at the foot of his bed. He could smell the coal and cigarettes, the cold winter air coming off him in waves. He wanted to talk to him, to hear his voice, but he was also afraid.

Another time it was Tilly—he'd know her perfume anywhere. And next Mr. Portman with Archie at his side, Mr. Portman with his head smashed in, Archie with half his body blasted away. They were saying his name in turns, each time louder than the last. Art. Art. Art. ART. He woke up shouting, the metallic taste of blood in his mouth, the acrid smell of gunpowder clogging up his nose.

And sometimes he saw other people passing through the room. A man with a white coat and a clipboard, a girl in a white-and-red striped dress. It dawned on him at last—he was in the hospital. He had no idea how long he'd been there.

He couldn't remember the last time he'd eaten or taken a drink—was that what these tubes running into his body were doing, keeping him fed and watered? His belly was swollen and sore. He was hot, drenched in sweat as though someone had poured a bucket of warm water over him. And then he was freezing, shivering, his teeth rattling so loudly he was sure he could be heard in the street.

And this, goddammit. A catheter.

And then one day he woke up and she was sitting in the chair beside his bed.

His heart stopped.

Was she real or another apparition?

A nurse came in and began fussing around him. He was afraid to turn his head back toward the other woman in case she was no longer there, so he stared at the nurse instead. She cranked up his bed until he was raised enough to have a drink of water, which felt cool as it flowed down his parched throat.

"And we have a visitor again today," the nurse said, nodding in the woman's direction. "And for once we're awake enough to greet her."

He turned slowly. She was there. It was her.

It was Rose.

Her long hair was streaked with silver and her skin was pale like parchment, and she was old now, like him, and yet in most ways she had not changed. She still had that posture he'd always thought was somehow French. She was still a great and rare beauty.

"Rose," he croaked, and he wondered if this was the first time he'd spoken since they'd picked him up off the street.

"Art," she replied.

"I'll leave you to it," the nurse announced, and she moved on to the next bed.

"Rose," he said. "How . . . ?" His throat was so dry. It hurt.

"Next of kin," she said. "You never altered your papers." And she reached out and touched his hand and he fell away from the room and into the gauzy darkness that was now so familiar to him.

The next time he came around the chair beside him was empty and he smelled soup. An orderly appeared. He cranked up Art's bed and placed a tray on his table.

"Let's see how much you can eat today," the man said, as though this was an activity that took place regularly. Maybe it was. Art wasn't sure.

"Rose?" Art asked. He felt a little better. He could lift a cup of water to his lips without shaking.

"That lady Rose is so nice," the orderly replied. His accent suggested he came from far away. "She was here earlier. Don't worry, she'll be back." He plumped Art's pillows and said, "Eat your soup," crossing his arms to show he wasn't going to budge until he saw Art lift his spoon.

Art ate his soup.

—

He woke up. Rose was sitting in the chair beside him.

He raised his bed using the remote, like the orderly had showed him. Cleared his throat.

"Next of kin," he said. "I never changed it. I'm sorry."

"Don't apologize," Rose replied. "I wasn't sure who to contact. Who you'd want me to contact. Once it became clear you weren't—well, that you were going to get through this— I decided to wait until I could ask you. I can call Peg if you want me to."

Art thought of his sister. He pictured her and Frank at his bedside. Peg with tears in her eyes, Frank with that look of disapproval. "Not Peg," he said.

"Who then?"

"There's no need. As you said, turns out I'm not dead. Not yet anyway."

Rose nodded. "I've been spending more time in Vancouver these days. We've got an apartment down the way."

Still with that lawyer guy. Maybe she'd managed to have a happy life.

"I'm sorry," Art said.

"For what?" Rose asked.

"I made you give up on me."

He hadn't meant to say it. He closed his eyes.

"No one ever made me do anything I didn't want to do."

Art smiled.

"Is that so? Because if I remember correctly, I had to convince you to marry me," he said.

Rose gave him a long look.

"I always wanted to marry you, Art," she said.

He remembered those long months when Rose was pregnant, growing big with life. How happy he'd been, how happy they'd both been.

He sank back into his pillow. His anguish was as fresh as though it had happened yesterday.

"All these years," he said, "I thought you hated me."

"Hated you? Why?"

"Because of what happened."

"Because of what happened?" she repeated.

"What happened to us," he replied. He wanted her to be the one to say it.

"Celeste," said Rose.

"Celeste," Art whispered.

"She left us, Art. She left us and we forgot how to live. But I never hated you. I loved you. She was ours. You gave her to me."

Art found he couldn't speak.

Rose reached into her bag.

"I brought you something," she said.

She pulled out a hat. A tiny wool hat. Forest green, with a little bumblebee made of black and yellow yarn hanging on for dear life. He'd recognize that hat anywhere, his mother had knitted it. She'd been so damn proud of that little bumblebee. Of the hat she'd made for her granddaughter. His daughter.

Rose placed it in his hands. "You probably don't have anything of hers, do you?"

He shook his head. He didn't have anything that had belonged to Celeste. But now he did.

"She left us," he said.

And then hot tears were streaming down his face. And he didn't feel embarrassed, he didn't feel ashamed.

Rose took his hand. "We did what we had to in order to survive," she said. "And you'll get through this now, Art. I know you will."

They sat together through the afternoon, talking. Rose told him she'd gone into the wine business, converting a whole tranche of her orchard land on the Naramata benches into vineyards. He made her laugh when he said he would have made a reliable wine taster, if only she'd thought to ask him.

When Rose left later that day, Art knew she wouldn't return. But that, for once, it was okay.

2007: The Royal Palace

THE ROYAL PALACE HOTEL was what once upon a time Art would have called a dump, the kind of skid row hotel that used to be common over in Gastown before the city began to clean itself up. It was probably historic, Art thought, though nobody in their right mind would think of it that way. This part of New Westminster still had a dirty old lumber-town feel to it, though the condos of Vancouver were encroaching, marching up the river bringing the fancy gyms and restaurants behind them.

To passersby, the hotel probably looked lousy, the paintwork faded, the windows dirty and crooked. But those windows offered Art, in his fourth-floor room, a view of the Fraser River with its barges and its booms, and he'd often sit there, watching the tugboats coming and going. His room was spartan—a narrow bed, a wonky bedside table with the Gideon's Bible wedged under one leg, a beat-up old wardrobe with door hinges beyond fixing, and a battered desk. When he'd arrived at the Palace after his stint in the hospital, he'd had nothing but the clothes on his back and a little green hat to call his own, and that had felt like all he needed. Though of course he'd since acquired other things, including his own coffee maker. Today, he had a box of cereal and a fresh carton of milk on hand, so he fetched the cracked china bowl he'd picked up for fifty cents at the Goodwill—the same pattern his mother used to collect but thought too precious to use—made himself breakfast and sat by the window, contemplating the day.

The long stint in hospital had been followed by a much longer stint in a residential rehabilitation facility that Art knew he'd been lucky to get into. It took him time to dry out, as though he'd been soaked through to the bones with booze. He'd been in bad shape—scrawny, malnourished, his skin faintly yellow like he'd been preserved in formaldehyde. And yet, slowly, he got better. His bones dried out. His phantoms faded.

After breakfast, he headed out for his morning constitutional. Monday mornings New West was full of busy, rushing people in their yoga gear and their business suits, but Art didn't care. He never ran into anyone he knew from the past, though over in the park he'd usually find one of his fellow hotel residents. On a good day, he'd walk for a couple of hours, past the Skytrain station and across the highway, down to the river where he could take a look at the log booms that crowded the water around Poplar Island. But today he managed only half an hour before turning back—the clouds were threatening rain and his back was nagging.

The hotel entrance from the street was narrow, below an old sign that read "THE R   L PAL CE." Inside, the uninviting lobby and to the left, the hotel bar, with its cracked red vinyl bar stools and walls covered in yellowing pine boards. It was all very retro, and not in a good way.

"What are your plans for today, Art?" Laurie asked. She was next to him at the bar, in the red ski jacket and matching toque she wore no matter the temperature, taking tiny sips of the beer Art had bought for her. He liked to help people out when their chips were down—when Laurie's mother died he'd bought her a Greyhound ticket to Prince George. You didn't want to sit too close to Laurie. But she was a good sort.

"Oh, the usual," Art replied.

"I'm busy," said Laurie, "very busy." They were all busy, all his Royal Palace pals. Art knew what was up, Laurie herself had given the game away the other night. She'd been almost asleep, sitting at the bar hunched over a drink, and Art had given her a nudge. Mr. Wu didn't allow sleeping at the bar.

"It's gonna be so great," she'd said.

"What?" asked Art.

"Your party," she'd replied. She placed a finger on her lips and shushed.

He was going to be eighty years old that weekend. Eighty. And the good people of the Palace hotel were planning a party. A big old-fashioned knees-up. Well, that was fine with him. He'd been known to enjoy a party.

Mr. Wu himself was behind the bar this morning; Billy the bartender had gone missing. When the news got around, half the residents had volunteered to work Billy's shifts but Mr. Wu declined the offers. "You're all alcoholics," he said. "Except you. You're an alcoholic who does not drink," he said to Art. And he laughed. For some reason Art couldn't quite fathom, Mr. Wu found the idea of an alcoholic who doesn't drink funny.

Mr. Wu poured hot water into a metal teapot and placed it and a mug on the bar in front of Art. Sometimes Art nursed the same tea bag for a couple of days, letting it dry out at night between uses, but today he was starting afresh. Mr. Wu reached beneath the bar and handed Art the newspaper. "Leave the crossword for me," he said, though he didn't need to, he'd been sharing his newspaper with Art for longer than either man cared to remember. Art never knew which paper he was going to get—Mr. Wu wasn't a loyal man as far as newspapers went. Very occasionally was it today's paper.

The *Province*. Art looked at the date. A copy of the *Province* that was ten months old.

Art didn't mind. A paper was a paper. He had a radio up in his room where he could listen to the news, and there was a television over in one corner of the bar. Some nights, when that old urge to order a Scotch or two or three grew too strong, he used the TV and the racket it made as an excuse to escape the bar. Not that he was the world's most perfect teetotaler. He fell off the wagon from time to time. But the key difference between now and back in the old days—some people might say the bad old days, but truth be told, Art had loved drinking, he'd loved drinking more than most things, at least for a time—was that now he was able to climb back up into that rickety wagon once again.

He used to be full of schemes, invest in this or that, land a job up north or down south. When he was in the hospital, giving up on those mad ideas had been part of what had enabled him to move on, to find a way to live that didn't involve sleeping in damp doorways. And it was amazing how much further his pension went when he wasn't drinking.

He began to read. He worked his way through the months-old news, the sports, weather, entertainment, classifieds, funnies. Births and weddings. He skimmed the obit column, in case he recognized any names.

And there. Halfway down the page. Frank Turner.

Frank Samuel Turner. Died 10 October 2006. Survived by his wife, four children, twelve grandchildren, three great-grandchildren. Funeral service: Friday 22 October, 11:00 a.m.

Ten months—nearly a year. His brother-in-law Frank had been dead nearly a year.

Peg. Art put the paper down and took off his reading glasses. His sister Peg.

Art hadn't seen her in almost twenty years. He hadn't seen anyone from his family since that day he'd asked Peg and Frank for a loan. And Art still owed them that money. He'd borrowed money and he hadn't paid it back. He heard his father's voice—he'd heard it every time he'd thought of Peg these many years—*borrowing money you can't pay back is the same as stealing*. Art knew, if he knew anything at all, that stealing from your own family is not a good thing.

Art had had a plan. It was simple—he was waiting for the day he could turn up on their doorstep with a bouquet of flowers and a cheque for the full amount he owed them. He'd visit as soon as he could pay them back. He'd never wanted to let Peg down. He didn't want to see that look on Frank's face ever again. He'd show up with a cheque and everything would be all right.

But he realized now, eighty years old save a couple of days, his brother-in-law's obituary on the counter in front of him, that it was highly unlikely Peg was sitting in her kitchen fuming over the fact that he hadn't paid her back. Art didn't care about the money he loaned to his friends at the Palace. He didn't care if they never paid him back; in fact, he knew full well most of them never would. Perhaps Peg had known this too—had always known it.

Five grand. Was that all it was? Five grand.

But he'd never been anywhere near able to pay them back. The day they gave it to him it had slipped through his fingers like sand. It might as well have been five million. And because of that, he'd stayed away. For all these years. Sometimes Art felt as though he was so stupid it was a miracle he was still alive.

Art looked across the empty bar. Laurie had left. Mr. Wu was out back somewhere, Art could hear him banging around. There was a pay phone behind the partition, on the way to the Gents. And Art's jacket pocket was full of quarters. He'd loaned his good friend Teddy ten bucks the other day, and Teddy—Unsteady Teddy, they all called him, with his shaky arms and legs—had paid Art back last night with a popcorn box full of buttery change.

Art levelled himself. The arthritis in his back and shoulders gave him grief, but it was worse in his hands, his fingers stiffened at odd angles.

He dragged a nearby bar stool over to the phone and stacked his quarters on the little shelf beneath it.

He knew Peg's phone number by heart.

He'd read a book about trees the other day. He went to the library most afternoons. They knew him there, they'd even made him Reader of the Month last year, put his picture up on the wall so people could ask him for book recommendations. No one did, but it was a nice idea, and he'd appreciated the gesture. He read all manner of books, but the librarians knew he'd been a logger, so they liked to lend him books about natural history, in particular books about trees. The book he'd read the other afternoon explained that trees in a forest are all connected via their roots, that the forest floor is a kind of communication network made of moss and insects and fungi and all manner of life, and the forest itself a single organism, like a living soul regenerating through an endless cycle of rot and regrowth. This information did not surprise him.

Art dialled.

It took a while for Peg to answer.

"Hello," she shouted, and she dropped the phone. He could hear her scrabbling around, muttering—"Hell's bells, where's the damn thing?" And then her voice was clear, and close once again. "Hello?" she said. "Is that you, Nancy? My hands are wet. Cooking." And she laughed her wonderful laugh and Art sat up straighter on his stool.

"Hello, Peg."

Silence.

"Peg?"

"Is that you, Art?"

"Yes."

"Is that really you?"

"Yes. How are you? How the hell are you?"

"Well I'm—I'm fine."

"I'm sorry about Frank."

Peg sighed. "He's gone, Art. Turns out you're there one day and the next day, you vanish. And you leave all your stuff behind."

"So I'm told. I'm sorry, Peg. That man loved you. You were lucky." He knew this was the truth now. He paused. "Listen. There's going to be a party."

"I beat you to it, Art."

"What?"

"I'm already eighty. I got there first."

"Damn. You were always quicker than me."

And Peg laughed, and they began to talk, interrupting each other, there was so much to say, and Art put more quarters in the ancient pay phone, and it was as though they'd been together just yesterday, and tomorrow they'd run down to the lake, leap across the burning sand and dive into the water.

And Art would hear the train on its tracks heading into town and he'd run home in time for dinner with his mother, his father, Tilly, Peg, and Eddie, and Archie was just across the street, and Rose was up the lake, everyone was with them, and anything was possible, and he could start all over again.

ACKNOWLEDGMENTS

This novel is loosely based on a bit of family history. Thank you to my siblings and our cousin Brian Low for their contradictory stories; all of our memories are reliably unreliable.

Thank you to my brother, Peter Pullinger, for multiple road trips around the Okanagan where he has lived for many years.

Thank you also to my brother-in-law Clyde Morrison (and his brother Ken), who grew up in a coastal logging camp and provided invaluable fact checking on logging terminology and customs. Of course, any errors are mine.

And thanks to my husband, Simon Mellor, for everything else.